EDIS...

and the
REPUGNATRONS

- LEE HODGES -

ISBN-13: 978-1479198894
ISBN-10: 1479198897

I wish to say a <u>BIG</u> thank you to Philip Ives for his fantastic illustrations!

Visit the website at:
<u>www.edisonfox.co.uk</u>

No aliens were hurt during the making of this story...

To Emma, for without your constant ~~nagging~~ encouragement, this book would still be gathering virtual dust in my virtual bottom draw...

Contents

An Infectious Breakout

Deep within the bowels of number sixty four Apathy Lane a red telephone rang. The headmaster of the St Commodore School of Excellence jumped, almost knocking it into the wastepaper bin along with class Thirteen's woeful homework. He'd been expecting this call and for a few moments he just stared at the phone, gathering his nerve.

With a deep sigh, he cleared his throat and lifted the handset.

'Ah, um, yes?'

'Mr Bruntingthorp?' said a brusque voice on the other end.

'This is he,' replied the headmaster, trying not to sound meek.

'Good. This is doctor Archimedes Mendoza Chuzzlewick. We spoke ten minutes ago.'

'Let me think,' said Mr Bruntingthorp, trying to appear so important that he could have received hundreds of other calls in the last ten minutes.

'Do excuse me,' cut in the doctor, 'I do tend to forget how common the name Archimedes Mendoza Chuzzlewick is. Do you need more time to remind yourself of our conversation or do you feel that you have adequate control of your ageing memory?'

Mr Bruntingthorp made to kick himself under his desk but connected instead with a crate of twelve year old malt whisky, which was meant to have been staff Christmas presents but now formed the backbone of his daily medicinal routine.

'No, I remember,' the headmaster admitted once his 'medicine' bottles had finished chiming from between his feet.

'Good. Have you brought the boy?'

'Yes but what, exactly, did you say was wrong with him?'

Doctor Chuzzlewick made annoyed noises in Bruntingthorp's earpiece.

'Literitis Horribilis.'

'I can't say that I've ever heard of that one...'

'And you being a fully trained doctor and all,' put in Chuzzlewick.

'But...how did he, you know, get it?' said the headmaster, now throwing a worried look in the direction of a rather unkempt looking thirteen year old sitting opposite him. A thirteen year old that was becoming increasingly concerned for his own well-being

2

the more of the headmaster's conversation that he listened to.

'Contact with books,' said Chuzzlewick. 'Ink to be exact; especially the old stuff. You know, like the classics. The ones that have been knocking around for some time. Anything by Shakespeare for example. What's that Midsummer's something or other? All that "blah blah blah", a worst offender that one.'

'I...I'm sorry,' stuttered the headmaster.

'Oh, not to worry, Bruntingthorp; not your fault. So, are you releasing him into my care or do we have to wait until the whole school is struck down because I assume you know what's worse than Literitis Horribilis?'

'Er, no; what?'

'Vocabulus Vomitus, and that's what it leads to when you leave it too long.'

'Oh cripes!' gasped the headmaster. 'But what about your phone number, I should really be checking on his progress?'

Sitting at the other end of the line with a Bluetooth earpiece and both hands darting across a computer keyboard in the darkness of his bedroom was not the celebrated doctor Archimedes Mendoza but another thirteen year old by the name of Edison Fox.

'Yes, of course you can have my number,' replied Edison, who was wearing a t-shirt that was enough to earn him a month of detention on its own.

Hacking into the British Telecom intranet site Edison located a suitable existing customer account and assigned them a second telephone number. He then re-routed all incoming calls to that number to his own mobile phone.

3

'Right, here you go,' he said and read out this new number. 'Now, can I speak to Master Cripps please?'

'Of course,' said the headmaster and he passed the receiver to the bewildered boy opposite, being careful not to make any skin-to-skin contact in the process.

'Uh, yeh?' said the boy into the receiver.

'Jimmy, it's Edison. You've been sprung. Grab your pencil case – the big job's on!'

> Five hours twenty-two minutes later, the Bon Café, Qual De Granelle, Paris

'So, do we have a deal, Monsieur Scratchit?' said Edison, staring across the table to where a rather large woman and her even larger husband sat grinning foolishly back at him. Billy-Bob and his wife were small time farmers from a forgotten corner of America who had for years tipped away the 'dirty water' from their cow shed until Billy-Bob was informed that the dirty water was in fact oil and that he was now a multi-millionaire. Fortunately for Edison and unfortunately for Billy-Bob, the farmer had "no idea how much a millionaire be..."

'Hey,' boomed Billy-Bob, 'this place is quaint, aint it just? Eh?'

'Yes, it is. Quaint,' agreed Edison in his best morose French accent, wishing the Parisian ground would open up and swallow him and there and then.

4

'Yep, I'm lovin' this place!' enthused Billy-Bob. 'Think I'll buy it, what d'ya reckon hun?'

The waiter, who appeared to be trying his very best to avoid approaching their table, shuffled over to them with a resigned look on his face.

'Excusez-moi, puis je prendre votre ordre?'

(*Excuse me, may I take your order?*)

'Hey, that's cute!' declared Billy-Bob. 'Er, what did he say, boy?'

Edison secretly typed into his electronic French translator, which he had hidden under the table; it was not reacting well to his shaking finger jabbing at its screen and he suspected it was giving him some rather bogus phrases but it would have to do.

'He is asking what drinks we would like – espresso's all around?'

Billy-Bob and Nancy had absolutely no idea what an espresso was but it sure sounded quaint so they nodded gleefully.

Edison tapped into the translator once again.

'Combien de vos clients sont morts?' he answered confidently.

(*How many of your customers have died?*)

The muscles in the face of the waiter shifted into a completely incomprehensible expression.

'Er, excusez-moi?'

Must be my pronunciation, thought Edison, *I'll try another.*

'Ce restaurant n'est pas aussi bon que le McDonalds!' he said with a smile.

(*This restaurant isn't as good as McDonalds!*).
The waiter threw a terrified look towards the serving hatch as the chef hurled a decidedly blue expletive through it. Sensing that maybe something had been lost in translation, Edison simply said, 'Café, café.'

(*Coffee, coffee.*)
The waiter gave a curt nod and shuffled off, taking the long way around to avoid passing the serving hatch.

'So Monsieur, do we have a deal? It's a truly fantastic property.'

'Well,' said Billy-Bob, 'it sure sounded awesome but I ain't seen it yet.'

'It's right there,' said Edison, pointing out of the window. 'I present to you Le Tour Eiffel - the Eiffel Tower!'

Billy-Bob and Nancy took a collective intake of breath that almost sucked the tablecloth clean out from underneath the condiments. Edison smiled in a devious way – the line was cast, the bait surely taken.

'Jeepers   Creepers!'   exclaimed   Billy-Bob.
'That…that's…awesome!'

'Awesome!' mouthed Nancy who, having lost the ability to conjure up her own words, stole Billy-Bob's instead.

'It's true, it's true; it is most awesome,' said Edison in what he considered to be an Oscar-winning display of wretchedness. 'I'll be heartbroken to see it go.'

The silence that followed was broken by the return of the waiter who placed a tray of coffee-filled cups onto the table whilst casting its occupants a contemptuous glare. Edison tapped his finger across the display of his handheld translator and turned to thank the waiter.

'Je pense que ce café a été bu avant!!'
(*I think that this coffee has been drunk before!!*)

The waiter gave them all a withering look that required no translation and turned instead to serve a new arrival.

'What do you think, Monsieur?' said Edison.

'Forty thousand you say?' said Billy-Bob. 'What's that in cows?' he asked his wife under his breath.

'Humm, about thirty acres worth,' she replied. 'But it depends.'

'What on?'

'How close they stand together...'

Billy-Bob sat and contemplated the proposal for a while, trying to wear a look that made him appear shrewd but only managing to look perplexed.

'I smell a rat!' he said finally. There was a scraping of chair-legs from behind them.

'I...I don't understand,' said Edison as a man in a smart suit rose rapidly to his feet and made his way over to the serving hatch. Edison placed his hand discretely into the pocket with his mobile phone and pressed a few, well practised buttons.

'Forty thousand dollars; it seems awfully cheap for such a big hunk 'o metal,' said Billy-Bob.

'Well, I am letting it go cheap to ensure a sale. My grandmother is really ill and if we don't sell it before she...you know...*goes*, the government will seize it and turn it into tin cans.'

'Hummm,' said Billy-Bob, rubbing the stubble on his chin.

Outside, a limousine pulled up and a person wearing a chauffeur's uniform three sizes too big got out. Edison excused himself and went outside to meet him. Billy-Bob and Nancy watched as the chauffeur said something to Edison and then placed his hand lightly on his shoulder. Edison appeared to go weak at the knees before nodding solemnly. Patting the chauffeur on the arm he made his way back into the café, ignoring an escalating fracas between the suited customer and the café manager.

'Are ya okay, little buddy – you seem kind 'a pale?'

Time to reel him in, thought Edison, his upper lip quivering in a tremendous display of distress.

'It...it's my grandmother; she has passed away,' said Edison, pulling out a handkerchief and blowing into it loudly.

'Well, I'll be.   I'm truly sorry about that, little bud. Hey – does that mean the deal's off?'
Edison fixed him with a calculating gaze.

'Well, not if you sign on the dotted line straight away,' he said, pulling out some "extremely legitimate" deeds and a pen within the blink of an eye. 'I could date it from yesterday when my poor, poor grandmother was still with us.'

Billy-Bob paused; Edison pushed the deeds and the pen closer, his heart seeming to skip several beats.

'Okay, little buddy, you've got yourself a deal!'

In Edison's head, a fanfare played out in triumph whilst behind them a commotion broke out in the kitchen.

'What do you mean, you're the 'elth inspector? Rat? What rat? There is no rat in my kitchen!' There was a strangled cry as four members of staff attempted to stop the head chef from bludgeoning the grey-suited health inspector with a large frying pan by jumping on top of him.

'I think it is time we were going,' said Edison. 'Our business here is done.'

As they made their way toward the door, Edison thought it only polite to thank the rather terrified looking waiter.

'il semble que votre chat est en feu!'
(*It seems that your cat is on fire!*)

Buy Now, Pray Later

Edison and Jimmy sat in Edison's bedroom, staring at the neat little bundles of cash spread out over the bed, and chuckling. Jimmy wanted to throw the money about like they do in the movies but Edison was having none of it – he liked order and a strict sense of control, not that you could tell from the state of his bedroom, which was littered with all sorts of cannibalised electronic gadgets and gizmos the use for which Jimmy could only guess at.

'And we are totally untraceable?' said Jimmy.

'Totally,' replied Edison.

Jimmy smiled, imagining all the things that he was going to spend his share on.

'Only I wouldn't want to hand it back now, I'm getting used to having it around. What're you going to buy first?'

'We can't go flashing it about,' said Edison, being typically sensible. 'People will get suspicious if we seem to have suddenly come into money.'

Jimmy pulled the same face that he usually reserved for his mother when she tells him he can't have any more pocket money.

'Maybe I could buy a new beanie, I've had this one for years,' he said, pulling his threadbare hat off of his head and releasing a tidal wave of curly black hair from underneath.

'I think that would pass as inconspicuous,' muttered Edison. His eyes flitted across a computer screen showing images from a French newspaper's website causing him to snigger wickedly. The page showed Billy-Bob Scratchit being led off by the police whilst Nancy, a wild look in her eyes, brandished a clutch of 'authentic property deeds.'

Edison sniggered once again before closing the web page. From within the centre of a table full of equipment came a buzzing noise quickly followed by an electronic ditty. Jimmy leant over and plucked Edison's mobile phone out and flipped open the lid.

'Looks like you've sold another piece of rope from Titanic's fishing nets. Did the Titanic ever have any fishing nets?'

'No,' replied Edison in a completely matter-of-fact way before loading up his eBay profile on the computer and checking out the sale. 'One born every day. Honestly; if I were to sell my mum's kettle and say it was from ET's spaceship, it would cause a bidding frenzy.'

'Hey, they're out there, you know!' insisted Jimmy, missing the point as usual.

'Don't start with all the "little green men" rubbish again.'

Jimmy knew better than to argue a point with Edison. Mostly he never won and, even when he did, he got that sneaking suspicion that Edison had planned it that way and that, in fact, he'd lost after all.

'Anyway,' said Jimmy, changing the subject, 'I was on eBay the other day and I came across someone selling off crates of bottled water really cheap. Thought there must be a scam in there somewhere if you were to buy some.'

'Really? Hummm, Holy Water from the Vatican...' mused Edison. 'Did you get the item number like I taught you?'

'Oh, yeh,' he said and pulled out a scrap of paper from his pocket, along with a month's accumulation of fluff and sweet paper wrappers. 'Ready?'

'Yep.' Edison dropped his computer's cursor into the eBay search box. 'Fire away.'

Jimmy started to read out the long line of numbers that identified the item from all the others in the vast eBay database. Edison typed them in with one hand.

'There's a number missing,' said Edison as Jimmy fell silent.

'I know, I can't read my own writing. The last one's either a six or an eight.'

'Well, it's a fifty-fifty situation. We'll go for a six, shall we?'

Edison hit the number six and clicked the search button. The website paused whilst eBay churned through its database to find the item before eventually opening a new page on the screen. Edison's eyes narrowed as they scanned down the page.

'Now this,' he said with an enthusiasm which was most unlike him, 'is definitely not crates of water.'

Jimmy managed to tear his eyes away from the piles of money and ambled over to Edison's desk. Edison began to read out the item description.

"Nuclear powered Neutrino Concentrator for connection to the subatomic intergalactic information superhighway. This is not the older AstroUplink Two Thousand (the one that had a tendency to run at temperatures of around six thousand degrees and would incinerate everything within fifty metres – including you) but the much better DataBlast Six Thousand and Twelve which never gets above room temperature, even when connecting to the infamous Lobster Nebula all the way over at sector G901. If it's faultless connection to the widest Universal networks available that you want, this is the equipment you need. Failing that, it makes a great talking point for dinner parties if placed on the mantelpiece."

Edison scrolled down the screen to where a small movie file was running on a loop. It showed an object that looked like a horizontal lava lamp with wire couplings at either end. However, unlike the limited colours found in actual lava lamps, this one contained what looked like rolling and writhing storm clouds which constantly

13

cycled through a mind-boggling array of the most indescribable colours that Edison had ever seen in his life. His eyes were drawn to this even more than the piles of money lying on his duvet and he knew there and then that he had to have it.

'I have to have it,' he said, not taking his gaze from the screen. 'Pity it's a windup,' he added with a sigh as the logical side of him won the battle between common sense and daydreaming.

'It's got to be – hasn't it?' said Jimmy.

'Of course, probably knocked that movie file up in Photoshop. Look at the sellers' online name – "Crackpot Joe", sounds really dodgy.'

'Sounds like one of your scams,' said Jimmy, moving closer to the screen and reading the detail for himself. 'Although, it does say payment on collection so at least you'll get to see it before you part with your cash.'

'True,' said Edison thoughtfully.

'Any bidders?'

'Only one, "Space Cadet Carl".'

'What's the price up to?'

'Nine pounds and thirty pence with twenty nine minutes to go before the end of the auction.'

'Go for it, it's not like you can't afford it.'

Edison thought for a short while before shrugging and grabbing the keyboard. Within a few keystrokes he had loaded up another website which acted as an automatic bidder when using online auction sites. Instead of sitting in front of your own computer and repeatedly typing in higher and higher bids, this system allowed you to type in your maximum amount before initiating a bidding frenzy on your behalf in the last few seconds of the auction. As long as your maximum price is high enough, then you're virtually guaranteed to win the item. This is why Edison always won auctions as his stored maximum bid was ten thousand pounds – plenty enough to win anything that he wanted on eBay. Edison entered the auction item code for the Neutrino Concentrator into the auto-bid website.

'Easy,' he said smiling, 'what could possibly go wrong?'

> Twenty-eight minutes and fifty seconds later, Edison's bedroom

'Well?' asked Jimmy from the bed, where he had taken to thumbing through the bundles of cash again. 'How's the bidding?'

'Still nine pounds and thirty pence,' replied Edison as he scrutinised the page before hitting the refresh button. 'Ten seconds to go.'

Jimmy joined him at the computer and watched the final seconds count down.

'Eight, seven, six,' counted Jimmy, 'five, four – still nine pounds thirty - two, one...'

Then a computer somewhere on the internet leapt in with Edison's bid of nine pounds and thirty-one pence. At this moment in time things were fine and would've stayed that way if a counter-bid of nine pounds and thirty-two pence hadn't been put in by the same auto-bidding computer on behalf of Space Cadet Carl. In that last second, this unseen computer went

15

into battle with itself, constantly bidding, being outbid and re-bidding ever higher and higher amounts for both Edison and Space Cadet Carl.

'Yes, you've won!' declared Jimmy one second later, doing a little jig on the spot. But Edison didn't answer; he was too busy feeling his face become numb. 'How much did you win it for?'

'Urm, well...bargain really,' said Edison, his voice thin and reedy. 'Nine thousand, nine hundred and ninety nine pounds and ninety nine pence...'

Jimmy looked at him with an astounded expression.

'*Real* inconspicuous.'

> One hour and twenty three minutes later, the dark end of Crowfoot Street

It may have been a cruel twist of fate that had caused Edison's pockets to be lighter at the end of the auction by nearly ten thousand pounds but his luck wasn't all out as the seller of the Neutrino Concentrator lived just a short ride away from Edison's house on the number forty-eight night bus. Having walked onto the bus with nearly ten thousand pounds cash and insisted to the driver that they still qualified for half price tickets, Edison and Jimmy hopped off twenty minutes later in an area that was so notoriously grim that the bus driver wished them luck before slamming down the accelerator and disappearing in a cloud of exhaust and tyre smoke.

'Are you sure we're in the right place?' whispered Jimmy, his eyes darting around all the dark

16

places, expecting a mugging at any moment. Edison squinted at the map on his handheld computer from where it sat hidden in the inside pocket of his jacket – no need to advertise themselves as targets, he thought, as he too gave a quick scan of their somewhat dodgy surroundings.

'Yes, number thirty-two.'

Seeing that the number hanging in two pieces on the door closest to them said "13", they began to walk cautiously down the street; caution being required mainly because most of the street lamps had been used for target practice and only every fifth one worked.

'Why do I have to carry all the money?' whispered Jimmy who looked around desperately as if he had just shouted "free cash!" Edison looked him up and down cynically.

'Let's just say you don't look the type.'

A dog charging out of an alleyway, knocking over several dustbins in the process, almost gave Edison and Jimmy heart failure. As it disappeared into the gloom, a determined looking ginger-tom gave chase just moments behind – even the cats were mean in this part of town.

As they made their way further down the street, the houses became more and more run down. Eventually they arrived at the ruin that was number thirty two. Its threadbare roof and crumbling brick walls seemed only to remain standing courtesy of the rampant ivy that almost covered the building. Only a few small windows were visible as an eerie red light seeped reluctantly out of them.

'Are you sure about this?' said Jimmy, throwing number thirty-two some seriously dirty looks. 'It's rather expensive for a lava lamp and I quite like being alive.'

'I know, but I've got a funny feeling about this; I think it's worth having. I'm sure we can come to an agreement on price.'

Edison walked through the gateway, the actual gate having been wrenched off some time ago and hurled into next-door's overgrown front garden. He passed an old rusting estate car sitting up to its door-handles in long grass; it had one wing missing, the windscreen was held in by sticky-tape and wedged onto the driver's seat was an old crate.

'Are you coming, Jimmy, or am I leaving you out here with the cats?'

Jimmy seemed to think about it for a moment or two before the howling cry of a fearsome feline terrified him into following Edison rapidly up the pathway, whimpering.

Stopping at the ancient-looking door Edison knocked on the layers of peeling paint. As his knuckles made contact, the section of wood beneath caved in, leaving a hole looking through into darkness. Edison glanced at Jimmy, who seemed to be preoccupied with scanning the building to ensure that all the knocking hadn't started a chain reaction of collapse. Edison looked back and gasped – which, by Edison's standards, was a shriek for anyone else – because staring back out at him from the hole was an eyeball. This eyeball seemed to flick back and forth, taking in the sight of them both before a voice spoke from the other side of the door.

'Who?'

'My name is Edison, and this is Jimmy. I won your auction for the Neutrino Concentrator. I've come to collect.'

'Ah! Yes, yes, okey-dokey-sure.'

There was a succession of snaps, cracks, clanks and creaks before the door swung inwards, something it was not at all pleased about having to do. Edison and Jimmy jumped backwards. From the darkness a short figure shuffled toward them. The owner of the roving eyeball was one of the oddest people that either of the boys had ever set their own eyeballs upon. Being no more than five foot tall, he seemed to have very little neck and, judging by the way he shuffled, either no knee joints or else unfeasibly stiff ones. Edison's eyes moved from his wispy white hair to his clothes, which looked like they came from a Rocky Horror stage show - presumably this was Crackpot Joe.

Crackpot wandered out a little way from the door, his face taking on a worried expression as he looked up into the night sky, which is not easy to do when you virtually no neck. After a few moments, he seemed to have satisfied himself about something and pointed his head and shoulders back in Edison and Jimmy's direction, smiling with what appeared to Edison to be an oddly wide mouth.

'Happy good-good. Come!'

Crackpot turned on the spot and shuffled back toward the house. Edison and Jimmy shared a look that spoke volumes but seemed to conclude very little and so followed in the man's awkward footsteps.

The inside of the house was almost as dark as the street outside. The same dim red glow that could be seen at the windows fell limply over the décor that time forgot. The wallpaper was only matched in its bad taste by the swirly, headache-inducing carpet.

Crackpot led them down a hallway packed with cardboard boxes. As Edison past, he noticed that some of the boxes were humming, some vibrating and others were emitting an odd glow from within. Crackpot reached in to an open box and pulled out an ornate vase which he offered to Edison.

'You like? Nicey, nice! Used to belong to Queen of Sheba! Old! Five hundred cash! Only one in world!' He turned to face Jimmy. 'You want? Nicey hat!' he said, staring intently at his beanie. 'Want swap?'

Jimmy looked affronted that anyone would try and part him from his beloved beanie hat. 'No! I've only got one!'

Crackpot shrugged and shuffled off through a seriously crooked doorway.

'You've got to give it to him,' said Jimmy, 'he's good.'

Edison turned the vase over and studied it.

'Not that good,' he said thrusting it into Jimmy's hands, 'it's a Royal Doulton.'

They followed Crackpot into the adjoining room where the little man was sitting at a rickety desk upon which was a computer so big and old that it took up most of the desktop. As Crackpot tippity-tapped on the keyboard, the computer hummed and rattled like an old central heating boiler and was probably giving off just as much heat. However, it wasn't the computer that caught Edison's eye, or even the strange way that Crackpot's hands seemed to stay perfectly still while his long fingers with their oddly purple fingernails jumped all around the keys, but rather it was the beautiful glowing object next to it – the item that he'd come to collect.

There's the nuclear powered Neutrino Concentrator, thought Edison.

'There's the lava lamp,' said Jimmy.

Over at the desk Crackpot had pulled up the online auction sale details. He laughed such a violent, cackle of a laugh that he almost rolled off his chair.

'He he! One born every day!'

Edison gritted his teeth.

'Jimmy, the cash.'

Jimmy reached into his pocket and pulled out the bundle of notes; now that Edison had seen the Neutrino Concentrator for himself, he was so captivated that it never occurred to him to question the sense in handing over so much money.

Crackpot pulled the Concentrator toward him and disconnected leads from either end, leads which looked to Edison to be plugged into the computer itself.

'Does it…er…work?' said Edison rather lamely seeing as he didn't really know exactly what it was that the device did, he just felt that he ought to ask.

'Work? Yes work. Work well. Powerful. Best money can buy! Would give demonstration but-' he cast the skies another worried glance through a grimy window, '-in hurry.'

21

The deal was done. Jimmy gave Edison the money who passed it to Crackpot. With a sense of high reverence, Crackpot slowly and carefully lifted the Neutrino Concentrator, its clouds rolling and shimmering in a million shining colours, walked toward Edison, and dropped it into a Tesco's carrier bag.

'Sold! Now, want buy kettle?'

Close Encounters of the Transferred Kind

The next day, Jimmy wandered into school as normal only to find his fellow students parting before him like the Red Sea. As he reached the main doors Mr Bruntingthorp saw him coming, screamed and slammed the doors shut, shouting "Get back to the clinic!" through the letterbox. Jimmy didn't need telling twice and with a shrug of his shoulders, ambled his way over to Edison's house.

'Bruntingthorp's off his trolley,' he said as he manhandled Edison's over-excited pet dog, Fleabag, out of the bedroom door. 'He's spraying down the pupils as they go in.'

Edison grunted in reply; he was sitting in the middle of a large pile of cables that he was attempting to couple up to the Neutrino Concentrator, but was having no luck in finding one that would fit.

'Anyway, what're you doing home?' added Jimmy.

'I called the school, explained that as the one that hangs around with you *all the time*, that I wondered what was up with you. They told me to see someone called Doctor Archimedes Mendoza Chuzzlewick and not to set foot in the school until I had a certificate of good health...'

'Oh. What're you up to?' Jimmy sprawled out on the bed, which didn't look like it had been slept in that night.

'Crackpot Joe had this thing coupled up to his computer somehow; I'm trying to find a lead that will fit.' He cast aside yet another incompatible cable. Jimmy let his eyes wander lazily around the room.

'What about that one?' he said, pointing at a table lamp in the shape of a little green alien. Edison rolled his eyes but he'd tried everything else. Unplugging the cord from the back of the lamp and taking the other end out of the power-pack, he tried it in the Concentrator.

'I don't believe it,' said Edison, 'a perfect fit! Just need to get the other end connected to the computer.'

Within ten minutes he had cannibalised a data cable from a printer and spliced it onto the other end of the lamp lead.

'Ready?'

'Whack it in,' said Jimmy. Edison carefully pushed one end of the cable into the data socket on the front of his computer. He turned and looked at the Concentrator – nothing, the clouds within were still rolling gently with a slow morphing of one colour into another, just as it had been doing all night.

'Never mind,' said Jimmy.

Edison rubbed his chin in thought but then activity on the computer monitor caught his eye - a message had popped up in the middle of the screen:

"New hardware detected: Nuclear Powered Neutrino Concentrator. Attempting to locate computer interface drivers…"

Edison held his breath. Another message popped up to replace the last one:

"Drivers installed; your new hardware is ready to use!"

Jimmy and Edison exchanged looks; Edison's was one of surprise, Jimmy's was one of incomprehension. Nothing new there then. Having no idea at all what the Neutrino Concentrator did for the computer, Edison turned to the internet for help — someone out there must know. He opened an internet browser window on the computer. No sooner had the page started to load then the Concentrator shook, settled and then hummed gently, the clouds now spinning and tossing within the confines of the glass device.

'Interesting…' muttered Edison.

'Sparkly!' offered Jimmy, staring at the entrancing lights of the Concentrator.

A short but dramatic tune announced the successful loading of the internet browser page. Edison's brow furrowed as he studied the text on the screen. For a second he thought he was looking at an eBay page but then he noticed some subtle, and some not so subtle, differences. For starters, the spinning logo in the top left corner was a three dimensional "gBay" symbol with what looked like shooting stars orbiting around its centre, the words "The biggest auction site in the known universe!" beneath it. In the middle of the page were links to items that looked like the contents of a Star Trek fanatics loft whilst on the left were some rather odd headings:

Transportation:
Battle Cruisers / Star System Grand Tourers / Shuttle Craft / Interceptor Discs / Alien ReCon craft / more…

Life Style Accessories:
Low Gravity Laser Tennis / Asteroid Billiards / Clay Comet Shooting / High Atmosphere Skiing / Moon Walking / more…

Home Accessories:
Food Replicators / 3D Holo-TV Sets / Cyber Butlers / 'Life Pause' Cryogenic Bed Chambers / HolTran Transporters / MatGen Transporters / Neighbour Neutralisers / more…

Edison smirked as he read down the screen.

'What's this site?' asked Jimmy, looking over Edison's shoulder.

'Someone's idea of a joke I think,' said Edison, clicking on an image entitled "Pet-o-Nator, the ultimate answer for stopping the K9 next door from peeing on your Astroturf!" As the information for the item loaded, a message at the bottom of the page appeared:

"Welcome back, Crackpot Joe; would you like to place a bid on this item?"

'Check it out,' said Jimmy with a chuckle, 'it thinks you're the weirdo that sold the Contemplator!'

'Concentrator.' Edison's face took on a smug look as he manoeuvred the mouse pointer over the "Bid Now!" button.

'Nine thousand, nine hundred and ninety nine pounds for a Neutrino Concentrator, eh? I hope that he *really* wants a Pet-o-Nator...'

He dropped the cursor into the box marked "Your Bid in GalCreds"

'How much do you reckon a GalCred is worth?' he mused to himself, assuming that he was unlikely to get a sensible answer from Jimmy. 'I'd say that Crackpot Joe would be happy paying one hundred thousand GalCreds,' he said, entering the amount into the web page and hitting the "Confirm Bid" button. As the screen cleared, it refreshed with the message:

"Congratulations, you are the current high bidder!"

'That should do it,' said Edison, leaning back in his chair and linking his hands behind his head.

'Yeh, unless a GalCred is like, totally weeny,' said Jimmy, trying to convey something really small by squeezing his thumb and forefinger together tightly and squinting.

'You're right.'

Jimmy smiled benignly, basking in a feeling that was mostly unknown to him - being right.

'Humm,' continued Edison, 'how to make life uncomfortable for our stumpy little friend? I know, I think it's time for Crackpot to make another sale...'

Edison clicked the "Sell an Item" button, skipped the "Large" option, the "Very Large" option and even the "Gigantic (collection only)" option before finally selecting the "Planetary or other celestial object" option.

'Impressive,' said Edison, 'these jokers have really done their homework.'

He manoeuvred the cursor into the description box and entered the following:

```
"For sale: a small blue planet covered mainly
in polluted water.  Quite new at around four
and a half billion years old but needs some
remedial repair due to being thrashed around
the solar block by its clueless inhabitants
(sold  separately).   On  the  whole,  a  good
runner.   An  abundance  of  added  extras  are
thrown in for free including Oxygen, Silicon,
Calcium  and  life-choking  greenhouse  gasses
but  the  real  bonus  is  the  vast  stockpiles  of
lethal  nuclear  waste  which  give  it  a  nice
green  glow  at  night.   Feel  free  to  drop  by
and check it out, it's parked just down from
Pluto and is the one that leaves a smog trail
as  it  goes.   Take  it  away  today  for  just  one
hundred GalCreds!"
```

Edison folded his hands behind his head and smiled.
'That ought to do it...'

The rest of the day slipped by uneventfully, if you don't count the havoc caused by Edison's dog, Fleabag, who had finally worked out how to open the bedroom door, meaning Jimmy had to keep throwing him back outside the bedroom.

'What do you think this dial's for?' said Edison, having discovered it hidden under a sliding cover on the Neutrino Concentrator.

'No idea,' said Jimmy, who was more interested in wiping Fleabag's slobber off of his hands and onto his school trousers.

'It must be a power gauge of some sort,' said Edison and he twisted the small dial to its maximum, causing the psychedelic clouds to thrash around like a ferret in a rucksack.

'That's upset it, that has,' said Jimmy who was regarding the concentrator with a nervous eye for it had now started to vibrate around the desktop so manically that an avalanche of paper slid off a shelf above and covered it.

'Better turn it down again,' said Edison and he reached under the paper and turned back the dial. The Concentrator calmed instantly.

'That's better,' said Jimmy, 'I thought it was going to go-'

BANG!

The lights flickered and crackled and a low frequency hum filled the room before fading out. In the hallway fleabag started to whine. They stared as a black object hovered momentarily in mid air just a few feet away from them before thudding to the floor. For a few seconds they simply gawped at the thing on the carpet – it looked like a chicken egg, painted black and with three rows of holes set at different levels.

'What-' started Jimmy.

'Don't know,'

'How-'

'Not a clue,'

'Where-'

'No idea,' said Edison, who had got over the initial shock and was now studying the object with his natural curiosity, albeit from a few feet away. Then without warning, an intense neon blue light shot out of the small holes in the object, causing Edison and Jimmy to shield their eyes until it had died down. When it had, they froze as before them stood two suited beings, each brandishing what any self respecting Trekkie would tell you was a ray-gun.

A metallic voice came from one of the visitors, presumably the one that raised its gun and pointed it directly at Edison.

'Go ahead, make my millennium...'

> The Bridge, Repugnatron Battle Cruiser, the dark side of the Milky Way

Gragnash, the supreme overlord of the Repugnatron Battle Cruiser, which was now orbiting a moon that strangely resembled an old prune, grabbed a long, rusty-looking lever with a gnarled, slime-coloured hand that strangely resembled a filthy squid and yanked it with all his might. It did nothing, but that didn't unduly worry him for he had absolutely no idea what any of the leavers did in the entire ship. However, this didn't stop him from yanking any that happened to come within arm's reach of his hover trolley, just as a show of authority. After all, if the other crew members thought even for a second that he'd no idea how to inflict pain upon them via some leaver or pulley, then he'd have been flung into the Grate-o-Matic and turned into supper centuries ago.

Suspecting that he was being watched out of the corner of one of a subordinate's four eyes, Gragnash hovered over to another lever and pulled that one too. Three hundred decks down, a junior Repugnatron toilet cleaner, complete with mop and bucket, was sucked out of a trapdoor in cubicle number sixty-six and vented into space. If Gragnash had realised, he'd have been most pleased with himself.

When it came to levers and pulleys, there was an almost inexhaustible supply on board Repugnatron Battle Cruisers. This was down to their irrational fear of technology. They understood levers. They understood pulleys. They even understood heavy, swinging clubs (the type full of wood, not dancers). They did not understand switches, they did not understand buttons and they most certainly did not understand keyboards.

However, a spaceship cannot be made from levers and pulleys alone and, disagreeable as they are, the Repugnatrons had been forced to make some compromises and some alliances – both things that they despised almost as much as computers - in order to heave their huge, collective bulks off of their planet and into space. The compromise was to install hateful technology into their battle cruisers but to put it out of sight, activated safely by pulleys and levers. The alliances were made in order to get hold of this technology and were with the Techonoids of Zeta Twelve, a race of tall, benign-looking creatures that could completely re-solder a computer's motherboard with one hand whilst writing out a list of races that they needed to annihilate with the other.

It doesn't matter how good your chef is - an alliance like this is a recipe for disaster...

'Lieutenant Fragnut,' said Gragnash in a guttural voice, 'have you found anything suitable in this sector yet or do I have to haul your miserable hide over the hull during re-entry again?'

Fragnut, who like all Repugnatrons resembled a pile of elephant droppings, zoomed his hover trolley desperately back and forth along the extensive range of levers and pulleys that disappeared first into a black box and then a Neutrino Concentrator, his slimy arms a blur. Just when Gragnash had produced a particularly gnarly looking club and was making his way toward Fragnut, the Lieutenant seemed to have pulled it out of the bag in time.

'S...sir, I got something; it's perfect for the job - and cheap!'

'Oh, really?' said Gragnash, and he belted him around what you might call a head anyway.

> Edison's bedroom, approximately 4.5 seconds after receiving unexpected visitors

To describe their visitors as "little green men" was a bit of a gross assumption and was probably politically incorrect in whatever part of the universe they came from. They were wearing what appeared to be a one-piece green shell suit and a helmet and weren't even particularly little, being around the same height as

Edison and Jimmy. Either way, they were making their presence felt and one of them had been skipping its diplomatic classes of late.

'Welcome t…to our planet,' stuttered Jimmy, giving a small bow.

'Shut it!' barked a metallic reply from the alien who had, up to this point, been pointing its ray-gun at Edison but now swung around to point it at a petrified Jimmy. Outside the door, Fleabag was going nuts.For a few moments Edison made no movements or any attempts at conversation. In his mind he trawled through a library-full of ever more ludicrous scenarios that would rule out the life-changing possibility that this was, in fact, an uncomfortably close encounter of the third kind. Having exhausted the library of options, the head librarian turned off the lights and kicked him out. Nothing for it then, he'd have to do something that seriously aggrieved him – he'd have to tell Jimmy for the second time that day that he was right, and had been all along.

'I'm not sure,' he said finally, 'what the etiquette is for this sort of thing but-'

'Silence!' snapped the one with the itchy trigger finger who then appeared to be scanning the room intently whilst staying rooted to the spot. It then turned and leaned close to its colleague. 'We need to find it before we can make a positive ID.'

Edison watched them closely, noting with interest how their helmets seemed to crackle with electricity where they accidentally touched and how, when they moved around, it was just a few footsteps from where they had appeared.

Suddenly the quiet visitor pointed over to the desk where a pile of paper was glowing gently. 'There?'

'You!' shouted the serenely challenged one. 'Move that!'

Edison frowned; he could see a pattern emerging here.

'Please, be my guest,' he said, moving aside to allow them access.

'Don't mess with me, I've got a Vaporiser and I'm not afraid to use it!'

A smile played across Edison's face. Putting his hand into his pocket he pulled out his phone and threw it at the quiet one.

'Eeeky!' it shouted as it instinctively went to catch the phone only for it to somehow slip through its fingers and onto the floor.

'Freeze!' shouted the other. 'One more move like that and I'm going to turn you to dust!'

'Whatever,' said Edison, shrugging in that way that only teenagers can manage, 'but I don't think you can, and shall I tell you why?'

If Jimmy and Edison could see through those helmets, they would have noticed a fleeting glance of panic between the two visitors.

'Because-' he continued but he got no further as Fleabag crashed in through the door and leapt across the room, his tongue lolling out of his mouth like the Red Barron's scarf. In one gulp he swallowed the black egg-like device on the carpet, taking with it what Edison had correctly predicted were the visitors' projected holographic images.

'That should buy us some time,' said Edison with a smirk whilst patting Fleabag on his head but Jimmy had opened the bedroom window. A whirring noise came in from the garden along with a couple of flashes of bright light.

'Erm, not that much time,' said Jimmy, sounding suddenly nervous.

'Why?' replied Edison, who had stopped congratulating a very pleased-looking Fleabag.

'Because our visitors are back — and they've brought their spaceship with them!'

Race Trace

Edison and Jimmy stared out of the bedroom window and down into the garden where despite nightfall, the shape of a highly polished silver disk could clearly be seen.

'That's original,' scoffed Edison.

As they watched, a brief glow of light showed from beneath the craft and their now familiar visitors stepped into view from the hidden underside.

'Now we're in trouble,' said Jimmy, 'they've put down on your mum's petunias.'

'Squashed flora I can cope with,' replied Edison, 'it's those Vaporisers that I'm worried about.'

Walking a little way out across the neatly manicured lawn, the two green-hued beings studied the house intently. One went to scratch its head in an outward display of concern but then realised it was wearing a helmet. The other shook its own head in exasperation before first pointing to Edison's window and then at its partner's belt. The other nodded in agreement and fiddled with a small device located upon it. Rising upward, it hovered just a few inches above the turf.

'Quick, they're coming!' said Jimmy as the two beings floated up toward them. 'Shut the window and hide!'

Edison couldn't be bothered to point out that any race capable of crossing galaxies would be quite competent at a simple game of hide-and-seek, and so with a sigh he walked calmly back over to his desk and tossed some chewing-gum into his mouth.

Jimmy watched in abject fear as the first being ducked smoothly in through the window and landed on the carpet. The second managed to crack its helmet off of the frame on the way in and ended up on its backside. For Fleabag, flashes of unnatural light were one thing but creatures flinging themselves in through the window was another so with a whimper he hid under Edison's bed.

'A personal visit this time,' said Edison, getting in first, 'we are honoured. So, who are you?'

'GPOL - gBay police, now shut it!' shouted the more surefooted visitor, who then stormed over to Edison's desk and threw aside the paper still covering the Neutrino Concentrator whilst levelling its Vaporiser at him.

'Ah ha! I knew it! It's game over, Crackpot; we've found you at last, despite your disguise!'

Edison shook his head. 'I'm sorry to blow a solar wind through your parade but-'

'Don't try and talk your way out of this one, Crackpot. GPOL have warrants for your arrest in three solar systems and this time we're not letting you slip through our fingers!'

'Do you want to tell them the bad news, Jimmy or shall I?' said Edison with a faint smile. Both of the visitors turned their helmeted heads toward Jimmy who could only manage a squeak, but this was because they had turned their Vaporisers on him also.

'I'm not Crackpot,' said Edison, who was acting as if aliens parked on his lawn and floated in through his bedroom window on a regular basis. The helmets and Vaporisers swung back toward Edison at this but then, after a pause long enough to make an obvious assumption, swung back toward Jimmy.

'No! No! Me neither!' stammered Jimmy. The two aliens exchanged hidden looks.

'Urm, do you think,' said the clumsy one, leaning toward its partner, 'that we should do a RaceTrace on-'

'Obviously!' snapped the other. Edison was not convinced that this one needed its Vaporiser with a mouth like that.

Lifting its gun arm, it waved a hand over a watch-like device on its wrist. In response, a shaft of neon blue light shone out from it like a funnel. Held suspended within this light were what Edison could only describe as icons, the type that you would see on a computer's desktop, but these were three dimensional and seemed to bob very slightly as if floating on water. The alien poked one of the icons with a finger, causing it

38

to move as it was 'virtually' pressed. A nice touch, thought Edison. All of the icons were then replaced by another set. The alien used this method to navigate through several levels before finding the option that it wanted.

'Right, stand still or I mean it - I will pump you full of antimatter!'

'Really?' said Edison. 'Can you use a small needle? I've a phobia...'

'Smart alec,' said the alien with a sly grin that, had Edison seen it, would have caused him some concern. Pointing its wrist device at Edison, a ray of blue light shot out, making contact with his feet. He felt a slight tingle as the ray of light was pointed ever higher up his body until it came to his head.

'Oh dear,' said the alien, 'looks like we have some interference here – must be particularly *thick* at this part...'

It twisted a virtual power gauge up to maximum intensity. Edison felt like he'd been thwacked with a cattle prod and made the appropriate noises despite himself. Under the bed, Fleabag was whimpering loudly.

'W...was th...that strictly necessary?' he demanded when the procedure had ended.

'For criminals like you, yes,' answered the alien who was now looking at the device as it displayed a three-dimensional hourglass.

'I am not a criminal - at least, not yours,' said Edison.

Suddenly the virtual hourglass disappeared and a three dimensional message appeared:

39

"Race determined as Human."

'So it would seem,' replied the alien in a shocked tone before it turned and repeated the process on a rigid-with-fear Jimmy.

'The same,' it said when the results had come through, 'I can't believe it, I was so sure.'

'What now?' said the other alien.

'Can you just be quiet for more than a few seconds? I need to think – and can you shut that creature up or do I have to neutralise it?'

That was it; Fleabag charged out from beneath the bed, threw up the "black egg" and jumped clear out of the bedroom window. A crash from below registered the partial demolition of what had once been a healthy rhododendron bush.

'Neutralise, not neuter, Fleabag!' shouted Jimmy out of the open window.

'Look,' said Edison, 'I'm quite sure that you have no authority here-'

'Read the small print, Neanderthal,'

'-and I think that it's clear that neither Jimmy or I are the person that you are seeking so if you don't mind I've got to do something more interesting like rearrange my sock drawer.'

The GPOL officer made to retort but a short trilling noise from its wrist device followed by the return of the blue funnel of light interrupted the response. Held within the light was a message:

"GPOL Unit 42: Urgent return to HQ to update on Crackpot apprehension."

The GPOL officer groaned and turned to its partner.

'Come on, we're wasting our time here. Pick that up.' It pointed at the slime-covered HolTrans device that Fleabag had just evicted from his stomach.

'Do I-'

'Have to?' finished the grumpy officer. 'Yes.' The device was lifted gingerly from the carpet like it was something odd, black and slimy, which it was. The two officers made their way toward the open window.

'This galaxy's a big place, but just you make sure you stay out of my way.'

'Missing you already,' retorted Edison.

After the obedient officer had fallen out of the window and destroyed the remainder of the rhododendron bush below, the second officer paused at the threshold and pointed its wrist device across the room, a beam of light shot out of it for the briefest of moments.

'Do you not even want to know where we got the Neutrino Concentrator from?' said Edison, trying to see where the beam had fallen.

'I think we can manage to work that out for ourselves,' answered the officer with scorn, 'but if there's anything important that you think we should know then now's the time.' The officer pointed its Vaporiser at Edison as if to prompt him into serious consideration.

'No,' said Edison.

From on the bed came a familiar buzzing noise followed by an electronic ditty. Jimmy's internal organs leapt upwards in unison. He calmed down, realising that it was just Edison's mobile phone. Picking it up, he flipping open the lid; there was a text message waiting. Jimmy clicked the "Read" button.

'What about you?' demanded the officer, who was now pointing its Vaporiser at Jimmy, 'Is there anything that you would like to tell me?'

Jimmy gulped, looked up at the officer and looked back at the text message:

"Congratulations, you've made a gBay sale! Planet Earth has been sold to the Repugnatrons for 100 galcreds!"

When he replied, his voice had risen to an almost inaudible squeak.

'No...nothing whatsoever...'

A Flash Delivery

'Wow,' said Jimmy, who was wiping his sweaty palms on his beanie. He watched as the gleaming craft lifted itself free of the petunia patch and shot into the sky with unbelievable speed. 'Now do you believe me?'

Edison didn't reply; he'd been left in very little doubt that their unannounced visitors were not exactly from around here, especially if their technology was anything to go by, and he was in no mood to admit it to Jimmy's face.

Just then another noise came from outside, this one grinding and shuddering. It sounded like someone driving something that they didn't have to pay the maintenance bills for. A few moments later, a dreadful performance of Elvis Presley's "Blue Suede Shoes" played out over three chords from the front doorbell. The sound of bolts being drawn back and a creak told

Edison that his mother had answered the door. There was a gasp, a groan and then the sound of Edison's mother shouting angrily up the winding staircase.

'Edison! What have you been up to this time? You had better go on up,' she said, talking to their latest visitors. 'Straight ahead at the top of the stairs.'

Jimmy and Edison listened as two sets of heavy-sounding footsteps made their way up the staircase. The door was flung open and blocking out the view to the hallway beyond were two grim looking men dressed in smart black suits. Both were wearing sunglasses and one had a box tucked under an arm.

'I knew it!' gasped Jimmy. 'It's the Men in Black! The government's secret agency for keeping the alien conspiracy quiet – they've come to wipe our minds, Ed!'

One of the men placed his hand into the inside pocket of his perfectly pressed black jacket, much to Jimmy's horror.

'You,' he said, looking straight at Edison with his one-hundred per cent UV protected eyes, 'over here.' Edison thought about ignoring the man but he looked like someone who could easily whip out his spine and use it for a xylophone.

Edison approached in his best "only doing it because I want to, not because you asked me to" walk. The man looked down at his t-shirt, smiled and nudged his partner who grinned widely.

Removing a device from his pocket that looked like a personal organiser, he held it out to Edison, who noticed that the hand gripping it had one too many digits.

'Spit on here,' he said, still smirking.

44

'Don't do it, Ed!' shouted Jimmy. 'They'll steal your mind!'

'We're not in the taking business,' said the man with the hi-tech spittoon. 'Now, spit. Please.'

'My mother taught me never to spit, it's rude,' said Edison.

'And my mother taught me never to bite the heads off of moon rats. A fat lot of good that advice was. "Study quantum mechanics", now that would have been good advice. Look where her advice got me.'

'At the risk of sounding stupid,' said Edison, 'where *did* her advice get you?'

'UPS. Universal Parcel Service - the delivery service for gBay. Flash and Gordon at your service!'

Flash - the man with the parcel - put his free hand into his jacket pocket and pulled out an ID card with the letters "UPS" printed in gold letters. He brandished it for a few moments before thrusting it back where it came from.

'Flash and Gordon,' said Edison with disbelief, 'you can't be serious?'

'Yeh, we love your movies, Earth boy!' said Gordon with a grin.

'So you're not here to take his mind?' said Jimmy.

'I wouldn't waste my time,' said Gordon, still brandishing the spit-machine.

Edison grunted, fished out his chewing gum from where it was sitting happily against his molars and slapped it in the middle of the device. The man in black couldn't look less bothered.

'That'll do nicely,' he said and Flash withdrew the box from under his arm and tossed it onto Edison's desk, narrowly missing his hand held computer. There was a tinkle from within as of something that would never be fit for purpose again.

'Is that it?' said Edison.

'Not yet. This one's cash on delivery. That'll be one hundred thousand GalCreds.'

'But I haven't even seen a GalCred, let alone have any.'

'We take a wide variety of payment methods. Galaxy Express?' Edison shook his head. The man's eyes settled on the open bag containing the remainder of the Eiffel Tower money. 'That will do,' he said, striding over and lifting the entire haul.

'No,' groaned Jimmy, 'not all of it?'

Gordon scanned the bag with his spittoon device -it was obviously multi-functional. 'All of it? No,' he said and pulled out a couple of loose notes. Jimmy let out a sigh of relief. The man handed the two notes to him. 'Here's your change.' Jimmy looked like he'd just eaten a three-week old cheeseburger.

With an unseen wink from Flash, the two men in black walked back out of the door.

'Oh, by the way,' said Gordon, waving the bag full of Edison's cash, 'your warranty's just expired. Have a nice day!' He pulled the door closed behind him with a shuddering crunch.

The boys exchanged startled glances before Jimmy ripped open the rather battered looking box. Two objects fell out: one was what looked like a cheap plastic trophy; it was snapped in two and had the words

"One billionth happy customer award, from your careful delivery company!" printed upon it. The second was a box with "Pet-o-Nator" written across it in jazzy lettering.

Looking at the box, Edison was unsure as to what it was that was causing him the most concern: the fact that mankind was very much "not alone" in the universe, or that he had been well and truly hoodwinked into giving all his cash away for an overpriced and probably broken item, the bill for which he had intended Crackpot to pick up - and if there was anything that Edison didn't like, it was being hoodwinked.

'What now?' asked Jimmy, 'do you think we should tell someone? MI5? FBI? SETI?'

'Call Fortean Times if you want,' said Edison dismissively, 'but I'm not letting this go so easily.'

'Letting what go?'

Edison was gathering various items together and shoving them into his pockets.

'Grab your coat,' he said, 'we're going. Now.'

'What? Now? Why now?'

'Because of this.' Edison held up his handheld computer for Jimmy to see, the screen was flickering and flashing wildly and pages of information rolled across the screen.

'It's crashed, it does it all the time,' said Jimmy.

'Maybe, or maybe that GPOL police alien scanned it, downloading all its information and causing it to crash.'

Jimmy looked like he was straining.

'No. You're going to have to help me out.'

47

'It had Crackpot's address on it. If they get to him before we do, then he'll be taken away and what's left of our money with him. One way or another, Crackpot has been responsible for robbing us of the entire Paris haul and I'm not letting him get away with it!'

Pet-o-Nation

> One hour and forty-five minutes later, the dilapidated end of Crowfoot Street

Despite Edison's determination to return to Crackpot's house, they didn't arrive in the vicinity until almost two hours after setting off. They had attempted to catch the number forty eight night bus but the driver had recognised them and slammed the doors closed, almost causing an unplanned surgical procedure upon Jimmy's nose. Apparently the boys' insistence that they stop at Crowfoot street the night before had given the locals enough time to set up a roadblock just around the next bend resulting in the bus's entire rear axle being liberated of its wheels. In the resulting confusion, they had even managed to reach in and take the driver's fluffy dice. He was not a happy man, something that Edison deduced from the energetic fist waving he gave them as he screeched away from the stop, leaving them to walk to Crowfoot Street.

'Strange,' said Edison as they approached the point where Crackpot's house should be, 'I've never seen weather this localised before.'

Just where the house stood was a bank of the weirdest fog that Edison had ever seen. It was odd not just because it was so dense that it looked almost solid but because it appeared to engulf the exact spot where the house should be and spread no further.

'I don't think we should go in, Ed,' said Jimmy, who was looking at the fog as if it were the entrance to Mr Yankem Ard's dental surgery.

'That money's not going to walk out by itself, Jimmy,' said Edison. He strode forward and was immediately lost from sight. Jimmy whimpered like a puppy before mumbling that the fog would at least hide him from the locals and sprang in after Edison.

As they made their way carefully through the gloom, they could hear a low humming noise that sounded like someone using a microwave oven; it echoed all around them but Edison could not determine exactly where it was coming from. Ahead, shafts of red light were lancing through the fog; this, he deduced, was from the windows and was good news – if the lights were on then maybe someone would be home.

A loud thud instantly followed by an "oof" told Edison that Jimmy had not been so careful to avoid the rusting estate car abandoned on the front lawn. He waited for Jimmy to retrieve his bag and reel off all the swear words he knew - which took time as some were used more than once - before reaching out an arm and pulling him to his feet.

'I realise,' said Edison with more than a hint of irony, 'that it's a bit late for this but please, be careful. This way,' he added, pulling Jimmy forward. 'There's a large shaft of light here, it could be the doorway.'

'Good,' said Jimmy, who was trying to rub his bruised shin as they went.

'Not necessarily; if it is the door then it's open, which in this neighbourhood in the middle of the night, is never a good thing.'

Moving slowly, they made for the light and found that it was indeed the front door. As they passed through, the fog stopped abruptly at the threshold, the return of their eyesight making them pause for a second to adjust.

The hallway was as it had been when they had last been there but with one difference – most of the boxes had vanished. Those remaining had been turned upside down, spilling their cheap and tacky contents out all over the equally cheap and tacky carpet.

'What do you reckon's gone on here?' asked Jimmy.

'Not sure,' said Edison frowning, he was kneeling down and pulling aside an empty box, beneath which he could just make out a faint red glow.

'What've you found?'

'No idea,' said Edison, who was turning around a small phial about the size of a hypodermic needle in his fingers, its luminous fluid content was moving slowly within like mercury.

51

Edison dropped the phial into his pocket and walked through into the room where Crackpot's computer had been set up. Besides the dusty and computer-less desk, the room was completely empty.

'I think we've missed him,' groaned Edison, 'he's done a runner.'

Jimmy had almost expressed how pleased he was about this when a bang from upstairs froze them where they stood.

'Do you think that's him?' said Jimmy in a whisper. Edison put up his hand to keep Jimmy quiet for more movements were coming from above. This time footsteps could be heard making their way across the loose floorboards. Not just one but multiple light feet, not the awkward shuffles of Crackpot.

Edison and Jimmy moved back into the hallway as the footfalls sounded on the staircase. Edison considered hiding but was convinced that the banging of his heart against his ribcage would give away his location in any case. Normally he wouldn't be overly concerned at this point but given what he'd seen over the last two days he could feel his stress-levels rising.

Then whomever it was reached the bottom of the stairs and became suddenly visible. Jimmy took an audible intake of breath; it was not Crackpot, it wasn't even an inquisitive group of locals out looking for abandoned wheels, what they were — for they were clearly not human — neither Edison nor Jimmy could say.

Fanning out across the hallway, blocking the exit, the beings scrutinised the two boys. They were tall, athletic looking creatures wearing body-hugging one-piece suits that glowed as if every strand of material were made of pure light. Their heads were too long for their bodies as if their craniums needed extra space in order to store a superior brain but their expressions remained blank and unconcerned - even when one lifted a complex looking contraption and pointed it toward the pair. Edison noticed that the creatures had what at first inspection looked like an extra long sixth digit on their hands but with shock realised it was an eyeball on a stalk, providing their brains with information as to what that hand was doing whilst the other hand could be concerned with doing something entirely different.

'It's life, Jim,' said Edison, disguising his trepidation with humour, 'but not as we know it...'

Suddenly, the device in the creature's hand shot out a beam of green light that took in every inch of Edison from head to toe. It then flicked to Jimmy and repeated the procedure. Edison took a step backward in surprise. The device started to howl as a red light flashed over and over. Edison might not be well versed in intergalactic convention but a flashing red light and a shrieking alarm always meant bad news, whatever star cluster you're from.

'Go!' he shouted and pushed Jimmy through the crooked doorway just as a bright white light shot out of the creature's device like a bolt of lightning. Crackling in the air, it shattered part of the doorframe, sending the two boys tumbling into the room beyond.

The boys struggled to get disentangled as dust swirled around them and large chunks of plaster fell from the ceiling above. They managed to clamber to their feet just as the creatures appeared at the now larger doorway.

'Behind here!' shouted Jimmy as one of the creatures raised its weapon, which was now making a whirring noise as if warming up for another shot. Edison felt Jimmy grab his arm and he was led in a spirited dive behind the now overturned desk in the corner of the room. As they landed in a heap, an explosion of bright light erupted where they had just been standing, sending chunks of busy wallpaper bouncing across the floor and wrenching an old gas fire from the wall.

'What now?' gasped Jimmy.

Edison's eyes flicked around the room taking in every detail – there was no escape. The doorway was covered and the window was stuck fast with decades of paint. As the lead creature at the door took aim again, Edison realised that they could not possibly miss a third time. He closed his eyes. This was it.

Edison's heart lurched as a loud crash filled the room, along with thousands of shards of broken glass and wood. He opened his eyes in time to see two figures running in through a huge hole where the window had just been.

'GPOL!' came a cry. 'Relinquish your weapons!'

Edison recognised the two green-suited visitors from his house, both of which were pointing their Vaporisers at the group of creatures standing in the doorway. But the creatures were clearly not in the mood to put down their weapons and come quietly. In the blink of an eye, two pointed their devices at the officers who, seeing the danger, fired their weapons in response.

As their vaporisers let out a blast of super-dense ion particles, an instant wall of protection sprang up around the tall creatures, enveloping them in a shimmering light. The blast from the Vaporisers ricochet off it and collided with the ceiling above their heads. With a terrific crash, the whole lot tumbled down upon the officers, covering them with debris.

The two GPOL officers struggled but were helplessly pinned under cross-members and floorboards. The tall creatures raised their weapons, lining up their sights as their weapons recharged for the next shot.

'Put down your weapons!' choked one of the officers but it sounded unconvincing and, quite frankly, hopeless. Edison's mind reeled; he couldn't just stand by and watch an attack on two defenceless beings, no matter where in the universe they came from. He looked around frantically for something - anything. His eyes found Jimmy's bag slung over his shoulder; seeing the Pet-o-Nator sticking out, Edison grabbed it.

'You know how to use that?' said Jimmy, staring at the device that looked like a cross between a lawn sprinkler and a tarantula.

Edison didn't have time to answer; he was just planning on throwing it at the creatures in the doorway as a distraction. As he glanced fleetingly at the alien gadget, he saw two controls: a dial and a button. As the creature's weapons were almost reaching their crescendo of recharge Edison cranked the dial round as far as it would go, hit the button marked "ON" and tossed it over the edge of the desk like a grenade.

As it flew through the air it lit up like a Christmas tree, emitting a skull-shaking wail as it went. The toss was good; it cleared the heads of the closest creatures and came to rest in the middle of the pack, whereupon it jumped up onto its legs, scuttled around in a circle before stopping and showering everything nearby with what looked like shards of molten metal.

The creatures in the doorway had suddenly lost their impassive expressions and were making noises of panic as they were assaulted by the Pet-o-Nator, which was scorching huge holes in the carpet. Then, in unison, they decided that enough was enough and pressing a button on the side of their weapons, they all dissolved into thin air.

'Are they gone?' said Jimmy.

'I think so,' said Edison, his heart still banging beneath his t-shirt. He climbed over the desk and hurried over to where the GPOL officers were trapped; one was finding it increasingly hard to breath and was making rasping noises. Edison started to pull off the debris as fast as he could whilst Jimmy did the same for the other fallen officer. When Edison had cleared all the beams and plaster he stood back, not knowing what else to do.

The officer didn't move.

Behind him, the other one was sitting up against the wall, moaning into the confines of its helmet.

'This one's not moving,' said Edison with mounting concern, he remembered how to administer

CPR from a first aid class at school but to the best of his knowledge, they didn't cover alien physiology.

Then the being's body seemed to spasm for a second before it let out a great gasp.

'Can't...breath,' it stammered and moving its hands to the bottom of its helmet, pressed two recessed buttons. A message warning of dangerous air quality projected itself from the officer's wrist device but was cancelled with a jab from a gloved finger. Edison jumped backward as a trail of blue light traced around the outline of the helmet's base before returning back to its starting position and fading out. The being placed two hands either side of the helmet and started to push upward. Edison took a further step backward, throwing Jimmy a look of trepidation – after the day he'd had, who knew what would be under that helmet?

As the Pet-o-Nator continued to throw molten sparks in through the doorway, the helmet slipped off with a hiss. Edison's eyes widened. As it came away, a tangle of dark, curly black hair fell loose around a young, attractive female face. A face so normal in appearance that, despite unusually dark eyes that appeared almost shielded, it could easily pass as human.

With an effort, the girl threw aside the helmet and took a few deep breaths before slowly turning her deep green eyes on Edison. In that moment, when their gaze was locked, Edison could tell from her solemn stare that this, here, was the first time that any human had ever seen these eyes. It was not something that she would have planned for but was powerless to avoid.

57

This was not supposed to happen. Nothing good could come of this.

Next to Jimmy, the other being also reached up and pressed its helmet's release buttons. Edison broke away from the girl's stare to watch as it lifted off its helmet to reveal a boy's face, complete with freckles and a mass of unkempt sweaty black hair. The boy let go of his helmet and yelled as it landed on his foot.

'It looks like we are in your debt,' gasped the girl, leaning up on her elbows. She winced as she tried to move her right leg, it had been struck by something heavy and was bleeding through her suit.

'That needs attention,' said Edison gravely.

'The suit will take care of the bleeding,' said the girl, 'but if anything's broken, it'll have to wait.'

As Edison watched, a grid of light appeared across the suit's right leg. In a matter of seconds it had located the gash and the other grid squares faded out, leaving only those around the wound; the light from them grew more intense as it went to work repairing the damaged tissue. Once the bleeding had stopped, the light faded out.

Edison made to comment but a warning alarm and a repeat of the air quality warning sprang up on the officer's wrist device again.

"Warning: Air quality compromised!"

'Must be all the dust,' said the girl, once again cancelling the alarm with a jab of the finger but Edison wasn't so sure. Glancing over his shoulder he

58

attempted to find the source of a hissing noise that he'd only just noticed.

'It smells funny over here,' said Jimmy, wafting his hand around in front of his face.

Edison looked down at the object that Jimmy was sitting on – a gas fire, its fractured pipe was hanging out of the wall, spewing gas past the dislodged grate and into the room.

'It's gas, Jimmy!' said Edison in alarm. 'Haven't you ever smelt it before?'

'No,' replied Jimmy, 'my house is electric!'

Edison was no longer listening; they had to move now before the Pet-o-Nator ignited two hundred cubic meters of gas and sent them all into orbit – without a shiny spaceship.

The Grate Escape

'Come on,' shouted Edison, 'it's going to blow!'

Jimmy and the boy didn't need telling twice, they shot out through the hole that used to be the window like scalded greyhounds. As the girl tried to get to her feet she let out a cry of pain, her leg giving way below her.

'It must be broken,' she gasped.

'I'll carry you,' said Edison who was now looking over at the Pet-o-Nator as if it were a stick of dynamite with a lit fuse.

'You'll never manage it, human,' said the girl through gritted teeth. Edison would normally have come back with some pithy remark but, given the circumstances, he cut the girl some slack. Besides she was right, working out at the gym was not Edison's bag.

Raising her arm, the GPOL officer started to navigate through the holographic menus one by one.

'That thing doesn't give off static does it?' said Edison; worried that it could trigger the mother of all suntans. The girl ignored him; she'd located the advanced medical functions of her suit and was selecting the 'Administer Pain Relief' option. She groaned as the pain in her leg subsided.

'We've got to leave,' insisted Edison. *'Now!'*

'Wait,' she snapped, selecting another set of options. Edison swore he could hear the beginnings of the combustion process from over in the hallway.

'If you select a "Make Suit Fireproof" option any time now,' he said, 'we're seriously going to fall out.'

'Just shut it and let me concentrate!'

As her fingers prodded at the icons, Edison could see that they were starting to shake, causing her to miss-select some, losing time as she had to go back and correct herself.

'Must be the pain relief,' she said, seeing Edison frowning at her. 'What're you doing here anyway?'

'A little business, just trying to return some money to its rightful owner.'

'How considerate of you.'

'Not really – I was returning it to *me*.'

'Even if your money's still here, it's about to be carbonised...'

Opening a 'Limb Isolation' menu, she prodded the 'Right Leg' option. As soon as it was selected, her leg shone with the same grid-work pattern before becoming completely immobile just as if it had been plaster cast.

'Now we go,' said the officer.

With her arm around his neck for support, Edison hauled the girl to her feet. Stumbling through the fallen roof debris, they staggered toward the hole in the wall, the sound of the escaping gas getting louder as they passed near to the damaged pipe. It was almost a relief when they reached the overgrown garden but Edison knew they were far from safe yet; if that gas went up they'd need to be well clear of the blast zone.

Outside Edison noticed that all the fog had completely disappeared.

'Over there!' said the girl, pointing to a silver disk dominating most of the large front garden, one of its three supporting legs resting on the bonnet of the old car. From behind them, a bright flash from the house burnt away the darkness as a pocket of gas finally ignited, throwing a blast wave of heat over them. In just a few seconds, the fire that was now raging in the living room would travel into the hallway and trigger the entire upper floor, roasting them all where they stood.

A platform descended from the base of the craft.

'Get in!' yelled the girl.

Edison stared at the craft and actually hesitated – was this really a good idea? However, the fire within the house was emitting a tremendous roar like a jet plane taking off and so he sprang after the others as they tumbled onto the platform. As soon as it had risen all the way, sealing the gap in the hull of the spacecraft, the two officers charged over to their seats, which were placed before a bank of large display screens, encircling the white interior like windows.

The girl was quick, despite her leg being rigid. She barked orders as she sat.

'Engines start...cloaking shields up...gravClamps off...'

With the last command, the entire ship shuddered and bobbed like a cork in a pond before settling.

'No way,' said Jimmy with a huge grin, looking around the space which appeared much bigger on the inside than it appeared on the outside, 'I can't believe they've let us in to a real-life spaceship!'

At this point it seemed that the onboard computer also could not believe that it had let in two alien creatures and so flashed them with a pulse of light, rendering their major motor responses useless. They both fell to the floor with a thud.

On one of the screens above the control console, the house was clearly visible; fire was belching out of the large hole that used to be the window. A flashing message appeared, warning that a catastrophic explosion capable of destroying the craft was likely within six point five seconds.

'Vertical clearance?' barked the girl at her partner.

'Clear!'

'Hold on!' she shouted. Edison wanted to know how, exactly, he was going to manage that given that the only muscular functionality that he seemed to have control of were related to basic life and dignity support only.

Grabbing a stick device that looked like it came straight out of the Nintendo test laboratories, the girl yanked hard backward with a grunt. This action was a little too drastic even for the flight-control computer, which failed to adjust the gravitational stabilisers in time. The two officers were thrust downward into their chairs whilst Jimmy and Edison were rooted to the floor so hard that Edison worried the platform would give way and jettison them out into the garden.

As the ship shot upward, all of the screens were flooded with an orange flare as the remainder of the pooled gas in the house caught, sending a red-hot shockwave chasing after the fast departing underside of the spaceship. The ship bucked and tumbled as the inertia controls struggled to deal with the teeth-shattering turbulence caused by the explosion but the girl hung on like a rodeo rider, pulling the controls fully backward whilst holding on to her seat with the other hand. To her right, the boy had his chair's support handles in a vice-like grip and was breathing in gulps.

As he lay on the floor, totally incapable of movement, Edison became convinced that it was getting hot. If he ended up with a permanent tattoo of mesh floor-panel across his face he would not be happy.

Then the jostling and jolting stopped, the flight evened out and all traces of fire disappeared from the monitor screens. They had ridden it out and were clear. Edison rolled his eyes at Jimmy who, although motionless, still managed to wink back. Edison knew that despite outward appearances, Jimmy was beaming from ear to ear on the inside.

From over by the controls, the girl was again barking orders to her partner who in reply was flicking and prodding switches rapidly. A warning message appeared on the screen above the controls.

'We've been picked up on air traffic control radar,' said the boy, 'they want to know if we're British Airways flight six forty five from Heathrow to Amsterdam!'

'Typical humans, three hundred tons of metal crawling across a wide-open expanse and they still manage to lose it. Give them a load of static and get us down again, we need to offload our hitchhikers.'

A few moments later, the ship touched down. Not that Edison or Jimmy would have realised as the computer had managed to get a grip on the gravitational stabilisers now that a certain female GPOL officer wasn't trying to rip the flight controller from the console.

'I need some fresh air,' said the girl to no one in particular as she retrieved what looked like a leg brace from a hidden storage area. She stepped over Jimmy, squashing his hand with her broken leg in the process (Jimmy made no sound but his eyes watered) and into the centre of the platform. Edison felt it move downward.

'You'll be okay in a moment,' she said, glancing down at the pair of them.

As the platform reached the ground and stopped, Edison felt an invigorating gust of cool wind rush over him. It was not quite daytime but there was a steely grey light in the sky and many unseen birds were starting to sing in anticipation of sunrise. The girl attached the brace to her broken leg; it looked too big at first but shrank to fit the limb perfectly. As soon as it

65

was on, the officer walked from the platform as if healed and made her way over a rise just ahead of where the spaceship had put down.

For a while, nothing happened to relieve Edison and Jimmy's paralysis. From a nearby bush a small rabbit scampered out and pulled up just short of Edison's nose, starring at him inquisitively. It was all Edison could do to engage in a staring match with the animal but the rabbit was having none of it and scampered off.

Slowly, Edison started to feel life return to his body. When he had the strength, he climbed to his feet. Next to him, Jimmy did the same.

'Wow! How cool was that? Did you see all those buttons! Do you think we made it into space? Is this another planet? How fast do you reckon we went?'

Not as fast as your mouth, thought Edison as he looked around for the girl.

'Where're you going?' asked Jimmy as Edison made off in the direction of the rise.

'One stratospheric death ride is enough for one day, I don't need a repeat performance,' said Edison over his shoulder. Jimmy grinned his trademark grin and went back up with the platform - he was not done with his backstage pass yet. If the GPOL craft had not been completely soundproof, Edison would have heard a thump as Jimmy was zapped into a smiling heap by the ships computer again.

Reaching the top of the rise Edison saw the girl sitting on the ground, her knees were pulled up to her chest and she had her arms wrapped around them as she stared out over the far reaching views from their hilltop vantage point. Sitting next to her, he followed her stare. From over the distant horizon, a pinprick of orange light spilt out over the lip of the world. Slowly it came, flooding gently over the landscape, glimmering from the surface of rivers and streams and embracing everything with its tranquil warmth.

'Are you okay?' said Edison; the girl looked like she'd been through a rough ordeal.

'You sound almost concerned,' replied the officer, not turning in his direction. Edison shrugged and looked back toward the horizon.

'It was a good bit of flying back there.'

'How would you know, have you ever seen anyone fly a GPOL Recon craft before?'

'I've watched Independence Day once or twice, you did as good a job as Will Smith. Although he *did* punch out an alien, which shows a flagrant disregard for the well-being of other life forms...'

The girl looked at Edison for a moment with a look firmly wedged between confusion and irritation before turning back to the rising sun.

'I suppose I should say thanks,' she said, begrudgingly.

'Thanks? Why?'

'You saved me back in the house. You didn't have to.'

'Did I? It was an accident, I didn't mean to. Rescuing is not my thing.'

'Thanks anyway,' replied the girl assuming Edison was joking, her expression now one of defeat. 'You had no reason, I'm not even one of your race.'

'Would you have left me there to die?' asked Edison; he was aware that the girl had turned her deep green eyes on him. There was a pause.

'No,' she sighed, 'I wouldn't have. Although, I'm under no obligation, you know,' she added, trying to claw back some sense of authority.

'Well, let's just agree that you owe me a favour,' he replied with a grin, always one to seize an advantage, although it was virtually impossible to see how this advantage could play itself out in future. The girl allowed herself a brief smile.

'What were those things trying to kill us back there?' said Edison.

'*Who* were those things?' said the girl sounding her shirty self again. 'Most advanced beings like to be referred to as "who" and not "what". That's the sort of thing that starts intergalactic feuds.'

'I stand corrected, please accept my ignorance of interstellar diplomacy,' said Edison. '*Who* were those things trying to kills us back there?'

'They weren't trying to kill us.'

'No? Really?' said Edison indignantly. 'Only there is - or rather was - a number of large holes in Crackpot's walls that say otherwise.'

'They were Technoids. They do have enemies in this galaxy but neither humans or GPOL are on their list. Yet. They were using stunning rounds; true they tend to react violently to matter not programmed into its stun spectrum but had they hit you, you'd only be temporarily incapacitated.'

'I feel so reassured,' said Edison. 'What were they doing there anyway?'

'Now that's something that I'd really like to know. As far as I'm aware, they've never ventured over to this part of the galaxy before. Something's not right and if we dig deep enough I'll bet we'd find Crackpot stuck directly in the middle of it all.'

'Any idea where he's gone?'

'We'll find him,' said the officer with a forced confidence.

'That'll be a *no*, then,' said Edison, earning himself a withering stare from the GPOL officer who then turned back and gazed at the steadily rising sun.

'It's beautiful here, despite what you're doing to it,' she said after a few moments, her voice quiet. Edison nodded, he was always far too engrossed in some crazy scheme to spare time for all this 'save the planet' stuff but now that he sat and took the time to appreciate it he admitted that it was.

'Where do you come from?' he asked. A spasm of emotion flashed across the girls face.

'We come from a binary planet that was twenty light years from here. It was beautiful also.'

'There's a lot of "was" in there,' said Edison. The girl didn't reply for a while but just tugged large clumps of grass from between her feet and tossed them into the breeze.

'It's all because of gBay,' she said at last. 'It's huge; bigger than you could ever imagine. It started off small, as these things do, but when the UniTrans was created — Universal Translator,' she added seeing the confusion on Edison's face, 'it opened gBay up to all civilisations, everywhere. Things went ballistic; in the early days just after the integration of the UniTrans the

69

whole thing almost collapsed under the strain and the best programmers had to be brought in to strengthen the system.'

Edison knew there must be a point to all this but thought better of asking her to cut to the chase.

'But all these new users meant more transactions and more transactions meant more dubious sellers passing on dodgy and often downright lethal gear.'

Edison cleared his throat guiltily at the mention of dodgy online sellers.

'Eventually gBay was getting more complaints than they could personally investigate. In response, a universal agreement was drawn up that gave authority to a group that would police the system, keeping an eye on known rogue traders, tracking down felons and bringing them to justice. Given the size of the task, the job was given to our race as a whole. It single-handedly cured the unemployment problems of our world as everyone was drafted into GPOL and given a patch. This meant setting up countless gBay space stations throughout the galaxies, huge flying fortresses that each house hundreds of thousands of our people.

'But that was our mistake. We left our planet unprotected. Can you believe it? An entire race of people dedicated to justice and protection and yet we left the back gate open.'

A blackbird in a nearby tree added its voice to the now clamorous dawn chorus, adding a note of cheer in a decidedly chill atmosphere.

'What happened?' said Edison.

'When we were looking the other way, a civilisation came past and ingested our entire planet for its energy deposits. Killing all those left upon it in an instant.' Edison was stunned.

'Recycling taken to its most unnatural conclusion,' he said in an undertone.

'It's no joke; do you actually know what it feels like to lose people you care about?'

'I lost my father,' replied Edison.

'Oh, did you?' said Ali, looking suddenly awkward.

'Well, sort of. I never actually knew him; I was very young.'

'What happened?'

'I don't know. My mother never talks about it but it makes her sad sometimes.'

'And you?' asked Ali. Edison pulled a dismissive face but did not comment.

'Anyway, what happened then?' said Edison, steering the conversation back to the original topic.

'Since then laws have been put in place to stop this sort of thing happening again. You need permission in order to destroy planets for their raw materials. It all came too late for my people.'

Edison stared at the girl; she looked like recounting this story had been the last straw in what had been a really bad day. And he thought school was bad.

'But there must be countless unwanted, uncared for planets out there that it would be okay to use, surely?'

'Yes but most of them are just rock and dust. Slim pickings when you have an entire civilisation to support.'

A silence came between them. The girl closed her eyes and let the amber light bathe her face. There seemed to be little comfort in it for her. Edison began to fidget; he was no good at awkward silences – especially when they involved girls. Then a noise of footfalls behind them broke the moment. Looking back, Edison watched as Jimmy came loping over the hilltop. Seeing Edison sitting there, he smiled broadly and stuck up both of his thumbs in a display that Edison took as meaning that he'd rather enjoyed his second comatose visit aboard the GPOL spaceship.

'So I assume you have some sort of names where you come from?' said Edison.

The girl gave him a considering stare for a moment.

'The one back in the ship is Perry, my name is Aliana. My friends call me Ali.'

'What do I call you?'

'Officer.'

'I see we've bonded already.'

'I must go,' she said, climbing to her feet. 'You can make your way home from here I assume.'

'What, no probes? No mind wipes? Not even a debriefing?'

'We could erase ourselves from your memory if we wanted but let's face it – who's going to believe you anyway? Goodbye,' she added and turned to walk away. As Edison stood, his mobile phone fell from his pocket and onto the grass. Picking it up, a frown

72

crossed his brow as he remembered a conversation that he'd had with Jimmy earlier that day.

'Hey,' he said, flipping open the phone's screen and walking up to Ali. She stopped and turned. 'Just out of interest, *who* was it that destroyed your planet?' She looked at him strangely for a moment before answering.

'The Repugnatrons, why?'

Edison handed over the phone; it displayed the message that confirmed the sale of Earth on gBay to the very same race. The colour drained from Ali's face.

'Oh no...' she stammered and ran for her ship, leaving behind a stunned silence that seemed to drown out even the birds.

Sold to the Slyest Bidder

The two junior GPOL officers sat in complete silence before the Admiral's desk, just the sound of humming from a translucent holographic monitor screen and the endless scratching of the Admiral's pen kept the silence from being absolute. The fact that nobody except the Admiral ever used such ancient methods of data capture as pen and paper made the wait even more frustrating. A short, round, balding man, the Admiral was the dictionary definition of 'overworked'. Despite the fact that there was not even the smallest scrap of paper anywhere in the rest of GPOL HQ, Admiral Titan still managed to have replicated piles upon piles of the stuff all around his room.

Eventually the Admiral applied a full-stop with so much force that the nib of the pen disintegrated, leaving a supernova of ink on the paper.

'Right,' said the Admiral, shoving to one side the holographic monitor screen and its depressing statistics of felons still at large, 'please tell me you've apprehended Crackpot...'

Both officers began to explain themselves at the same time.

'Erm, well, you see-'

'What you've got to understand, f-'

'Quieten down. Now,' the Admiral looked at Ali, 'officer GP232-' the use of the girl's ID number and not her name seemed to sting her like a wasp, contorting her features for the most fleeting of moments, '- it really is a simple question and could only have one of two responses, just one of which is what I want to hear.'

Ali took a deep breath and lowered her stare to the floor. When she spoke, her voice was slightly tremulous.

'No. *Sir.*'

'No,' repeated the Admiral with a deflated look, which only seemed to upset Ali further. He looked between the two officers, grave disappointment chiselled into his tired features. 'Can you at least explain why?'

Whilst Perry twiddled his fingers and studied the ceiling, Ali described their entire meeting with Edison and Jimmy, how Crackpot had sold his Neutrino Concentrator on the human online network and how he'd fled his last known address leaving a Technoid scouting party in his wake.

'Technoids, you say? Why were the Technoids this far out?'

'We're not sure but there's something else - the Repugnatrons, sir.'

All trace of expression fell from the Admiral's face for a moment before it became decidedly grim.

'What about them?'

> Back on the Bridge, Repugnatron Battle Cruiser, just off the horizon of Pluto

'Lieutenant Fragnut,' shouted Gragnash. 'Status report, now!'

'Err, what do you mean exactly, almighty overlord?' replied Fragnut.

If it were possible, the ugliness of Gragnash's face increased as he frowned with confusion, not even he knew what he meant, he just knew that most decent Repugnatron Battle Cruiser captains were always asking this question and he thought he should try it out.

'Erm, that planet,' he said in a rare moment of being up to date with current affairs, 'what's it called...Urk, are we there yet?'

'Ah, you mean Earth. Yes very close now, almighty overlord.'

'On screen!'

Fragnut hovered his trolley up to a large view screen that was akin to a dirty great eye and pulled a lever. As he did so, all the celestial bodies between the Repugnatron Battle Cruiser and Earth shot across the screen until the blue planet filled the display. Gragnash manoeuvred his trolley over to the screen and looked at it out of the corner of his four eyes whilst squinting uncomfortably. He was quite happy with the simplistic qualities of levers but there was no getting away from the fact that a view screen was pure, evil technology.

'Ah, she's a beauty, Lieutenant!'

'Indeed she is, sir!'

'Plenty of organic life forms?'

Fragnut pushed and pulled a few more levers and in response some Repugnatron characters appeared on the screen, making Gragnash flinch like he'd been laser-whipped.

'Ooh yes, sir – billions of crunchy life forms!'

'Excellent,' said Gragnash with a gleam in his quadrupled eye arrangement, 'the Birthing Pool is almost dry.'

The Birthing Pool was a tank around the size of Westminster Abbey that contained all the siphoned off bio-matter that their assimilators ingested when it swallowed a planet whole. The Repugnatrons would throw the odd body part, often taken forcibly from a smaller, more junior member during a bar-fight, into the festering quagmire of putrid filth and await the growth of a new member of the family. This new member would not so much be born as flushed out through the Large Artefact Drainage System when a blockage was detected...

A hailing noise from a cunningly disguised speaker system broke Gragnash's drooling and sent him into nausea-inducing panic.

'By the Stagnating Cheese Mountains of Halitosis Major, Lieutenant - what was that?'

'It was an incoming communication signal, sir,' said Fragnut whilst rolling his four eyes to himself.

'I know, I meant...err...ahem...Who's calling?'

Fragnut pulled a few more leavers, a smile stretched across his lumpy face.

'You're going to like this, sir.'

'Who is it?'

Fragnut told him.

Gragnash liked it.

> Admiral's Office, GPOL Headquarters, Milky Way Sector

'So, let me get this straight,' said the Admiral, 'this stupid Earthling has taken unlawful possession of a gBay licensed object, he has deliberately applied unsanctioned equipment to it and he has posted a sale auction for his *own* planet on the gBay network and now that auction has been won by the Repugnatrons and they are undoubtedly on their way to collect. Is this right? Did I miss anything?'

The two officers looked at each other dolefully.

'No, sir.'

'No, that's about the size of it, sir.'

Admiral Titan groaned, put his head in his hands and tried to rub off the last remaining strands of his hair.

'So what do you expect me to be able to do about it?' he said in exasperated tones.

'We have to stop this!' said Ali. 'Before it's too late!'

'But officer, you know as well as I do that all sales through gBay are legally binding. As much as I hate to admit it, the Repugnatrons are breaking no laws.'

'But you hate them,' she said, getting to her feet and balling her hands into fists. 'We *all* hate them!'

'Yes, and with good reason, but we have a job to do and we have to work within the parameters of the law. Please sit down.'

The Admiral typed a few words into a holographic keyboard that seemed to appear on demand below his virtual monitor and within seconds, a fact file on planet Earth appeared on the screen. 'I don't know why you're bothered anyway,' he said, gesturing at the information, 'they are primitive and potentially threatening to the stability of the galaxy.'

'But we only have the boy's word that it's a proper sale — shouldn't we at least challenge the Repugnatrons? Ask them for proof?'

The Admiral stared long and hard at the girl before him; it was true that if he thought there was even the slightest loophole that would throw a spanner in the Repugnatrons works then he would want to be the one that threw that spanner — or at least, be the one that pulled it out of the toolbox.

'Ok,' he said finally, 'but don't get your hopes up.'

Returning to his keyboard, he pressed a button that made the entire back wall of the office turn into a monitor screen. Upon that screen, a three dimensional representation of the Milky Way appeared. A few more keystrokes told the computer to look for the signature emitted by a Repugnatron Battle Cruiser. A line passed from one side of the display to the other like an air traffic controller's radar. The computer zoomed in on a blip in a sector of the map which showed the Repugnatron craft just passing the orbit of Pluto. At the press of another button, the display changed to a communications portal with a "Contact initiated, awaiting acceptance" message flashing in the centre. All three exchanged glances before the screen finally changed and the ugliest face this side of the Puss-Ball Nebula appeared.

'Ah, Admiral Titan,' came Gragnash's gurgling voice, 'it's been too long.'

'Not nearly long enough, Gragnash,' replied Titan, making no effort to keep the contempt out of his voice.

'For what reason do we owe this tedious intrusion on our time, Admiral?'

'Let's just cut to the chase here – where are you going in this sector?'

'Ah, just a little light shopping, combined with a refreshment break. That's all.'

'You're going to destroy Earth, aren't you!' demanded Ali. 'You have no authority!'

'Quiet, officer,' said the Admiral. 'Well, Gragnash, have you any proof of purchase?'

The lumps, bumps and boils on Gragnash's face reorganised themselves into a Repugnatron smile.

'You want to see proof? Well, if you insist...'

Gragnash extended his arm dramatically and grabbed hold of a nearby lever. With a theatrical flourish, he yanked it toward him.

'Here you go, proof incontrovertible!'

As the lever clunked into its new position, an alarm bell sounded. Five hundred decks down, the entire team of Repugnatron chef's were sucked up and pumped, in little pieces, into the dish of the day.

'Err, almighty overlord, it's not that lever – it's that one,' said Fragnut, pointing gingerly to the one next to it.

'I knew that,' said Gragnash and he pulled that one also.

On the Admiral's wall screen, an electronic document appeared, overlaying the view of the Repugnatron bridge. It was the gBay sales invoice for planet Earth.

'There you go Admiral,' declared Gragnash with a smirk. 'All legal and above board. Sold, to the highest bidder!'

'It's true,' said Admiral Titan with a sigh, 'it has the official Holo-logo.'

'It must be fake!' shouted Ali.

'The logo cannot be faked. The gBay servers cannot be manipulated. There's nothing we can do.'

'That's right, Admiral,' drawled Gragnash, 'nothing you can do, now why don't you go home and take a break – oh, sorry, you can't can you? It seems "home" has been destroyed somehow!'

Titan made an uncharacteristic snarl and threw his ink pen at the screen, it stuck in the wall just where Gragnash's head had been seconds ago but now was wobbling up and down in the centre of the line "Transmission terminated by the remote host".

'Damn those foul creatures,' muttered the Admiral as he attempted to regain his composure.

'There must be something we can do, sir; surely?' said Perry, almost pleadingly.

'Listen the pair of you, there's nothing you can do. Let it go. This planet is no real loss to the universe. There are plenty of lawbreakers out there that need your time and attention. You'd better go.'

The two officers climbed heavily to their feet, the Admiral was already scribbling away on another document with a new pen, the subject clearly over.

'At least,' he said without looking up from his work, 'you need not worry about chasing Crackpot any longer. He's on a sinking ship and there's no way he's going to barter his way out of this one.'

Ali paused halfway out of the door; a fierce determination had set itself into her expression at the Admiral's words. This was not over yet and no matter what, Crackpot would be singing like a bird to her questions. Or at least he would be if she could find him...

> Edison's bedroom, England, planet Earth, teatime

Edison lounged at his desk with his feet perched between two keyboards. In one hand was a generous helping of chicken dipper starters and in the other was the evening edition of the Daily Tribunal. Edison chuckled to himself as he scanned the headlines: "County Demolitionists Gazumpped As Bad Case of Gas Makes House Hot Property", "Bus Drivers Tire Of Tyre

Taking Tyrants", "UFO Eyewitness: 'Martian Marauders Mashed My Marigolds'"

'I can't believe people actually get paid to come up with these headlines,' said Edison as he tossed the paper into an overflowing bin. Jimmy grunted through a mouth full of food. Edison was quite happy that Jimmy had finally shut up; by the time the two of them had walked back home from where they'd been deposited on the hilltop, Jimmy had managed to chatter incessantly for hours on just about every subject even loosely connected with aliens. It was like watching the X-files box set on fast-forward.

As Jimmy finished off the food, Edison flipped open his mobile phone and stared intently at the gBay message that seemed to have caused the GPOL officer such shock.

'So, she just took off when she saw that text message?' asked Jimmy as he wiped his face with his sleeve.

'Yes,' said Edison, still in deep thought.

'Do think that it's true what happened to their planet? What if these Repugnant Matron things are going to do the same to Earth?'

'I seriously don't think so,' scoffed Edison, but deep down inside he couldn't help but wonder if Jimmy was right. He had no reason to think that the girl was lying about the Repugnatrons and the evidence was starting to point to the fact that the gBay system was, despite his thinking it was a joke, very real.

'You don't think they'll be back, do you?' said Jimmy.

Edison was about to say that GPOL would probably have no further interest in them once they'd realised that they were not Crackpot when Blue Suede Shoes played out in the entrance hallway. More visitors. Edison tutted; over the last few days, his house had seen more business than a Starbucks coffee shop.

From downstairs they heard the noise of security locks turning and the voice of Edison's mother as she opened the door.

'Good evening, how may I be of help to you?'

Edison and Jimmy strained to listen but could only hear one side of the conversation.

'Really, dear, you will have to be more specific, I really cannot deal in equivocality.'

'Your mum speaks funny, Ed,' said Jimmy.

'That sounds like my Edison,' continued Edison's mother. 'He hasn't tricked you out of your skateboards has he? Never mind, just go on up and get them right back.'

There was the sound of feet climbing the stairs and then the door was pushed open. Edison and Jimmy watched in astonishment as the two GPOL officers entered the room, still in their suits but this time without their helmets.

'The front door, that's conventional,' managed Edison, who was still a little taken aback by the officers' return.

'Hey, where's your spaceship?' blurted Jimmy, who stuck his head out of the window and looked down at the garden. 'Ed, there's two round dips in your lawn and your birdbath's as flat as your mum's Yorkshire puddings.'

Ali looked suddenly guilty.

'Urm, sorry about that.'

'I wouldn't worry,' said Edison, 'since they saw the size of our new cat the birds have been taking showers instead.'

Jimmy was still pointing excitedly into the garden.

'It's cloaked, Ed! Invisible! How cool's that!'

'Stealth mode!' said Perry, who was grinning as widely at Jimmy and as if joined on the same mental level. Both stuck their thumbs up at each other at the same time. Edison groaned – one Jimmy was bad enough, but two?

'I'm sure,' said Edison turning to Ali, 'that you didn't come all the way back here just to destroy our garden ornaments and if I'm not mistaken, you have that "cap in hand" look about you. Out with it.'

'If by that you mean it looks like we need your help then yes, we do.' Ali looked genuinely upset that this was the case. Edison smiled and leant back in his chair, hands clasped behind his head - this was a moment that he felt he had to milk for as long as he possibly could.

'More help? It would seem that we're not so inferior after all.'

'Look,' said Ali, her face hardening, 'help, don't help, see if I care – it's your planet they're going to destroy this time! Come on Perry, let's go, we're wasting our time here.'

Jimmy looked like he'd accidentally jammed his fingers into a live electrical socket.

'Our planet? Destroyed?' was all he could manage with an expression that would have had most of Harley Street reaching for their Mysterious Medical Maladies almanacs.

'So I take it that you've been back to your – Jimmy, help me out here.'

'Mother-ship,' put in Jimmy.

'- your mother-ship and have checked up on the Repugnatron thing and have established that I have, indeed, sold planet Earth to them, albeit without meaning to.'

'Yes, black-hole for brains, you have!' said Ali.

'Well, can't you just go and tell them the deal's off?'

'No.'

'Why not? You're the gBay police, aren't you?'

'Yes, but it's not that easy!'

'But why?' said Jimmy, who was having trouble adjusting to the thought of life without cheesy B movies, chicken dipper starters and, well, life. Edison held up his open palms in an 'I uphold the fruit-loop's question' sort of way.

'Because it's the law! All sales are final!'

'But you administer the laws,' said Edison. 'Can't you just make up some more?'

Ali made frustrated noises.

'Of course not. New laws have to be agreed by all races that are part of the gBay Code of Conduct and this includes the Repugnatrons. I can't see them signing off something that will lose them a good sale, can you?'

'Especially if it seems to help *your* race to stop *them* from doing something that they want to do,' said

Edison astutely. 'After all, there can't be much love lost between you lot.'

Ali was caught off guard for a moment and seemed to be battling between giving a GPOL response and launching a personal tirade.

'Our entire race,' she said after a deep breath, 'is committed to providing a professional and unprejudiced service to all, no matter who they might be.'

'Humm, straight out of the GPOL training manual I suspect, but tell me,' said Edison, leaning forward and holding the officer's gaze, 'do you actually care about our planet and its people or do you just want to get one over on the Repugnatrons?'

'I care!' she said with a ferocity that suggested to Edison that maybe she actually meant it. 'Of course I care.'

She went quiet and looked away. Edison realised that she had been playing with a necklace, which was almost unnoticeable around her neck.

'But,' she continued, 'I would be lying if I said that it wouldn't feel good if we smacked them right where it hurt!'

'And where exactly would that be on a Repugnatron?' asked Edison, raising his eyebrows.

'I was talking metaphorically,' replied Ali, but she was powerless to disguise a slim smile at the thought of her, a steel toe-capped moon-boot and a terrified Gragnash.

'Ok,' said Edison, rubbing his temples; they'd been talking their way through an entire litre bottle of cola and two packets of biscuits but they seemed to be getting nowhere. 'Let's go over the facts again. In the eyes of gBay, GPOL and the Repugnatrons, I have sold earth to the latter.'

'Correct,' said Ali.

'There is nothing within the law that can be done to stop the sale being upheld?'

'No.'

'Your Admiral is of the opinion that we're a lost cause and will not allow any more resources to even attempt to stop this happening?'

Ali nodded in an almost apologetic way.

'And you have come back here to ask us for help?'

'Yes.'

'How and why?'

'The "Why" is the easier part,' said Ali. 'We want to find Crackpot; something tells me that he's got more to say on this whole subject but I just can't work out why. As for the "How", absolutely no idea. I hoped you'd have some input there.'

Edison steepled his fingers and put them to his lips in an impressive display of deep concentration.

'Implants, Ed,' said Jimmy, who was still somewhat agitated at the impending destruction of Earth. 'Aliens always stick 'em in people to keep track of them!'

'Well?' said Edison, looking between Perry and Ali. 'Can't you just scan the entire globe for one of these implant things that you've stuck up Crackpots nasal passage?'

'Number one,' replied Ali shortly, 'we don't go around thrusting tracking implants into *anything* that moves – just those with criminal records. Number two, they're put into the leg, not the nose.'

'And does this change things with Crackpot?' enquired Edison.

'No on the first one, yes on the second...' said Ali.

'Explain,' prompted Edison with a quizzical expression.

'Crackpot has form,' said Perry.

'Which means that he was given a tracker,' picked up Ali.

'So you can track him, yes?' said Edison.

'Well, no. Not exactly,' said Ali, who now shared a grimace with her partner. Edison sighed – this was like pulling teeth. Not that he'd ever done that but if he hadn't an irrational phobia of all things dental then he would expect it to take him this long to pull a mouthful.

'Why?'

'Well, saying that implants are put in the leg is only half true. The fact is that they *used* to be put in the leg but now they are put in the-'

'Nose!' declared Jimmy triumphantly.

'-brain,' finished Ali. Jimmy huffed to himself.

'In fact, Crackpot is quite proud that it was he that forced GPOL to change this particular policy. You see, Crackpot is a Salamanderine. A Salamanderine,' continued Ali seeing the vacant expression on Edison and Jimmy's faces, 'is a being that can grow back just about any part of their body at will. So, he decided-'

'- to cut off the leg with the tracking implant in it and grow back another,' said Edison, shaking his head in disbelief.

'Yes, he did,' said Ali sheepishly. 'Look, we all make mistakes, at least we learnt from ours but if we don't find him then you may not get the chance to learn from yours!'

'So what you're saying, in a very round-about way, is that your technology is no good for the job of finding Crackpot?'

'Yes, I suppose I am,' said Ali sounding dejected.

'Well that's great,' moaned Jimmy. 'Maybe we can try going through the phonebook, someone must've seen him though it may take a little time ...'

'Ok, enough of the sarcasm,' said Ali.

'Hey, Ed, are you going to let her speak to me like that?' asked Jimmy but Edison didn't reply, his eyes had suddenly glazed over at Jimmy's sarcastic comment.

'Are you okay?' said Ali. 'Haven't you got any stupid ideas or are you just going to stare into space until it's blocked out with Repugnatron Battle Cruiser?'

'Jimmy's right,' said Edison in an undertone, his attention still taken up in thought.

'I am?'

'He is?' said Ali.

'Yes.'

Jimmy was beaming. He was on quite a roll lately.

'Well, sort of,' added Edison.

'Your turn to explain,' said Ali. Edison seemed to snap out of his stupor.

'You say that Crackpot has been selling items on our internet auction sites as well as gBay?'

'Yes, so?'

'Well when we were at his house before he left, he had a computer there.'

'Again, so?'

'If he's been using an Earth computer to gain access to an Earth-based computer network, he probably had a phone line.'

A gleam crept into Ali's eyes.

'And I deduce,' continued Edison, doing his Sherlock Holmes bit, 'that he'd avoid using a land line and would be accessing the internet via a mobile phone instead.'

'And this can be traced?' said Ali, her face a picture of suspense.

'Are Spock's ears pointy?' said Edison.

'That's a yes, right? Tell me that's a yes.'

'Oh yes,' said Edison with a look that only came of a new challenge. 'Fire up the hard drives, Jimmy, we've got a perpetrator to find!'

Reaper Seeker

Edison pulled his chair up to his desk and flexed his fingers above his computer keyboard like a concert pianist. This was what he enjoyed most; this was what life was about - the thrill of the chase! Okay, it was usually money that he was chasing but this time he would make an exception. After all, it's not every day you get the chance to impress interplanetary life forms, and Crackpot did owe him.

'So what are you going to do?' said Ali, standing next to him.

'Well, it's going to be a little complicated so take care to concentrate,' replied Edison. He didn't look up from his monitor to show Ali his sarcastic grin, resulting in him missing out on seeing her scowl, which would've burnt his eyebrows clean off.

Edison's fingers darted over the keyboard at lightning speed; only occasionally did he break away in order to use the mouse.

'Ok,' he said after a frenzy of activity, 'the first thing we need to do is find the number that Crackpot has been using to dial onto the internet.'

'But we've scanned your primitive communications systems before,' said Ali. 'There's millions of mobile telephones in use at any one time!'

'True, but you have to think a bit smarter.'

Ali's hand actually moved for her vaporiser at this point, fortunately for Edison she had left it back at the ship.

Edison logged onto his eBay account.

'The way to make this thing a whole lot easier is to firstly see when the advert for the Neutrino Concentrator was actually submitted to eBay. This will give us an approximate window of connection for Crackpot's phone.'

On the screen, he opened the purchase details for Crackpot's Concentrator and noted down the upload time. Ali looked at the purchase price.

'Nine thousand, nine hundred and ninety nine pounds and ninety nine pence – is that a lot in your currency?'

Edison closed his eyes for a second in order to let the moment pass without comment. Sensing that Jimmy was going to make some damming remark, he held out a warning finger to him without even looking in his direction. Jimmy risked making an 'I told you so' noise in his throat.

'The next thing we need to do,' Edison went on regardless, 'is click the link for the seller's information and see what else he's been selling. This will give us some more times that we can use to cross-reference and reduce the odds.'

He did this, bringing up a list of sold items under Crackpot's account. Jimmy stared at the screen with amazement.

'Genghis Khan's axe, Marilyn Monroe's false teeth, Van Gogh's vase of dried sunflowers – Ed, this guy's almost as good as you!'

Edison ignored this display of insolence and, clicking on the link to each item, he again noted down the times that these items had been added.

'Right, that should be enough. Next we need to find what mobile phone companies have cells in the area where Crackpot's house is, err, was.'

'What's a cell?' asked Perry.

'A cell is an area that is marked by phone masts that broadcast a signal between the phone company and mobile phones. It's a bit like a grid pattern, meaning that you can track a phone call down to an approximate place based upon which masts are picking up the signal from the mobile.'

'I knew that,' said Jimmy.

No one was convinced.

After just a few moments on the internet, Edison established that only one company were brave enough to put up phone masts in Crackpot's neighbourhood.

'Great, only one company,' said Edison. 'Skittish TeleCon, – this makes it much easier.'

With a speed honed through years of experience, he hacked into Skittish Telecon's servers and located all mobile phone connections that were made through that particular cell during the time that the Neutrino Concentrator was uploaded. Hundreds of numbers appeared on the screen. Ali groaned.

'Patience...' said Edison.

He then cross-referenced this list with results from the times of the other items that Crackpot had uploaded. The list dropped down to just ten.

'Wow, that's better!' said Perry.

'Ah, but wait for the icing on the cake,' said Edison. 'The other hunch I've got is that Crackpot doesn't own a contract phone - it'd be too hard for him to get through background checks. Instead I'm guessing he has a "Pay and Use" SIM card, which makes you effectively anonymous.'

Edison then got the computer to strip away any phone numbers that belonged to contract phones. It left just one on the screen.

'Ah ha!' exclaimed Ali. 'We have his number!'

Edison looked rather smug.

'Yes, but it's not over yet. Now we hope he has his phone with him and that it's on. That being the case, we need to track it to whatever cell his phone is currently in – if any. After all, I don't think he'd answer it and tell us where he was if we called.'

'Well crack on then, human,' said Ali patting his shoulder. 'I can smell those Repugnatron's from here.'

Crackpot kicked closed the door to the warehouse with a clang, cutting off a few tendrils of thick fog that had ventured over the threshold from outside. In his right hand was metallic device that had a large number of wires hanging from it whilst in his left was a folded piece of paper. He muttered as he waddled across the warehouse floor, passing the dusty and forgotten remnants of a long since closed fairground.

'Jolly jolly happy good, smooth like plan. Hurry hurry.'

When he reached the furthest, darkest corner of the warehouse, he stopped before a circular attraction that had a large silver ball in its centre. A sign that hung above it said: "Space Trek Waltzers" whilst below were numerous open-topped flying saucers with seats in them. As sure-footedly as a mountain goat on roller blades, Crackpot stumbled onto the waltzers and squeezed passed the little flying disks. Stopping at the large round ball, he held up a hand and touched the silver surface. The entire ball glowed before a hatch opened in the side, presenting a doorway.

'Yippy skippy; still worky good. Inside inside.'

Crackpot stepped through the hatchway and into the silver ball. The interior was small with just enough room for a seat, some controls and a view screen. On the floor just behind the chair was a small hatch and it was this that Crackpot threw open, causing an explosion of wires and leads to be ejected in a way

96

that only the manufacturers would be able to put back correctly.

An electronic voice sounded from somewhere within:

'Warranty invalidated!'

Crackpot waved the voice away in annoyance.

'No not return warranty forms anyway,' he replied and unfurled the piece of paper that he'd been carrying. On the paper's surface were many little diagrams with arrows pointing to various other diagrams and with little stick men demonstrating how to carry out various tasks relating to the metallic object in his other hand.

'Ikeacaramba!' he cried, staring in confusion at the paper, which he was now turning around and around in an attempt to work out which way would cause it to make most sense. 'How to put together? Buy cheapy cheapy, get cheapy cheapy!'

After a good few minutes of rotating both the instructions and the metallic object and staring at them with a completely bamboozled expression, Crackpot finally made a breakthrough with his cognitive efforts.

'Ah! Understandy! "Plug connector 'A' into receptacle 'B' and tighten", yes yes! Soon fix spaceship and be gone from stinky planet!'

As Crackpot's head and shoulders disappeared into the workings of the spaceship, a beeping noise came from within his pocket.

'What noisy?' he said, his voice echoing strangely from below. Leaving his head and shoulders down in the ships intestines, he fumbled around in his pocket with a free hand, eventually pulling out his mobile phone.

'Low battery,' he concluded, as the device beeped again, 'must turney offey, not need no more...'

> Edison's bedroom, dusk, almost suppertime

'Okay, so now we have his number and we're hoping his phone is switched on,' said Ali, sounding agitated, 'but how do we find him?'

'Relax,' said Edison, 'I have a plan, although this is the risky bit.'

'Risky how?' said the officer, with a frown.

'Risky as in if we mess up, an MI5 helicopter will unwittingly land on top of your invisible spaceship dashing any remaining hope of salvaging the birdbath, drop off a confused bunch of secret agents who will then storm the house and tie everyone up before throwing us into a dark cell for lengthy interrogation at a later date. If there are any later dates, that is.'

'Oh. *That* risky,' said Ali.

'Erm,' said Jimmy, 'do you think that's a little too risky?'

'What, more risky that hoping that the Repugnatrons run out of space-petrol before their Battle Cruiser reaches Earth and grinds it into its component molecules?' said Edison.

Nobody argued that one.

'Good,' he said, returning to his keyboard. 'Then let's get on with this. Now, what we're going to do is firstly hack further into Skittish TeleCon's systems and see if we can trace Crackpot's phone's journey through their cell network, this will give us an approximate location for where he is.'

'Approximate?' said Perry.

'Yes, the cells can cover quite a large area so we may only be able to pin him down to an area tens of miles square.'

'That would take too long to search by hand!' said Ali.

'Indeed,' said Edison, who was already passed the Skittish TeleCon's firewalls and into the inner sanctum of their server banks. 'Nearly there,' he added whilst running a program to show a simple diagram of the United Kingdom on his monitor. The diagram was criss-crossed with interconnecting lines that represented the cell structure, making it look like a honeycomb. At the bottom of the screen a cursor was flashing; Edison typed in Crackpot's phone number and pressed the enter key on his keyboard.

No sooner had the number been entered than the honeycomb display started to light up in sections as the Skittish TeleCon's computers searched its cell database for old and active connections relating to that number.

'Here we go,' said Edison; he was pointing to a highlighted cell on the screen, 'this is where Crackpot's house once stood.'

As they watched, the cells below them started to light up one by one as the system traced his journey southward through the phone network.

'Yes; keep going...' prompted Ali, whose fists were starting to tighten at the thought of getting them around Crackpot's neck.

'He's going south,' said Jimmy as the cells lit up one by one.

'Way south,' added Edison.

Just when they could go no further without ending up in the sea the trace stopped, flashing in the southernmost cell on the map.

'We've got him!' exclaimed Ali excitedly.

'Not just yet,' said Edison. 'Now we need to find exactly where he is within that cell.'

'I want a visual,' demanded Ali.

'This isn't Star Trek; it's just not that easy.'

'Whatever it takes,' insisted Ali, staring at Edison in a way that said the matter was no longer up for further discussion. Edison sighed.

'Ok. I can get the Skitish Telecon servers to work out his position but a visual is going to make things a whole lot riskier.'

'How?' said Ali, who felt like zooming down there and zapping anything that was shorter than five foot tall with her vaporiser.

'We're going to hack into a government spy satellite and get it to look for him.' Edison turned to his friend who was gawping back at him. 'Jimmy, open the vault, it's time for the Grim Reaper ...'

It took a few minutes to calm the commotion that was caused by revealing this part of the plan but eventually Edison managed to call order by banging repeatedly on his desk with his cast iron model of the U.S.S Enterprise.

'Look, are you sure you know what you're doing?' said Ali.

'Have you got any better ideas?' countered Edison, who was getting a little tired of being questioned. 'I didn't think so,' he added, seeing the officer's face lapse into submission. 'Jimmy, have you got that virus disk yet?'

Jimmy opened up the small safe that was hidden in a place that no one would think to look – under the bed – and using a finger and thumb as if it were actually infectious, plucked out the Compact disk containing the Grim Reaper virus.

'What does the Grim Reaper virus do?' asked Perry as the disk was dropped onto an open drive tray - he too was casting it a wary glance.

'The way it works is to provide a multi-layered software firewall that smashes through the one on the servers you're going to hack and then blocks any attempts to let them see what you're doing on their system. Because it has five layers, it doesn't matter if they manage to counter-hack through one or two because you've still got enough left to get your job done and get back out in time.'

'So what's with the "Grim Reaper" tag?' asked Ali.

'I agree it would be more appropriate to call it the Onion Virus due to its multiple layers but let's face it, it doesn't sound even nearly as cool.'

'But Ed, how're you going to get into the government systems from here – they are locked tighter than your mum's whisky cupboard. I remember reading once about this man who wanted to know who killed JFK and thought he'd try to-'

'Well, that's where I'm smarter than your man,' interrupted Edison, who didn't think it wise to let Earth go to the crusher just so Jimmy could finish his conspiracy story. 'True, the government are sitting there just waiting for someone to try and gain access to their systems over the internet or even for someone with a bit more enthusiasm to actually enter the building and plug in a laptop, but doing what people expect is not my style.'

'Listen, Neanderthal,' interjected Ali, 'your style is about to become crushed, siphoned and reconstituted – does that suit you?'

'Okay, keep your hair on. This is the plan: I'm not going in over the net, or even physically. I'm going in over their heads. Way over their heads. I'm going to firstly take control of Skittish TeleCon's telecommunication satellite from over the internet – their security's not a patch on the governments – and I'm going to turn it in space to face the spy satellite which sits above the United Kingdom. When it's facing the right direction, I'm then going to communicate with the spy satellite through its own communication array, which is a small disk that usually points in the direction of the next spy satellite in orbit – this is so they can talk to each other and send spy information around the curve of the planet. When in, I can upload the virus and take control.'

'Are you still talking?' growled Ali. 'Get on with it!'

A few short seconds later, Edison had linked back into the Skittish TeleCon's servers and had taken control of their communication satellite. Using its onboard mini-thrusters, which allow small adjustments to the satellite's position, he turned the dish away from its current direction pointing down toward England and had it spin around to its left instead. At this point, thousands of people all across the country had their phone calls cut instantaneously.

'How do you know when you're pointing that thing in the right direction?' said Perry.

'Simple,' said Edison, 'I just wait for the Skittish TeleCon satellite to receive an answer to its hand-shake protocol...'

Everyone looked at each other in an 'I've no idea what that meant but don't ask him to explain,' type of way.

'Bingo!' said Edison. 'The spy satellite comms are up. Jimmy, push that CD tray in, it's time to upload the virus.'

Jimmy pulled a face and trying to maintain a healthy distance from the virus disk, stretched out his foot and kicked the tray into the computer. Once the CD had span up and the program had loaded, a graphical representation of the virus structure appeared on Edison's computer screen. It did indeed look like an onion with each layer drawn in yellow circles getting ever smaller with the fifth layer being almost a solid circle in the centre. A message on the screen prompted the user to press the "S" key to send the virus to the host machine, which is exactly what Edison did.

'Here we go, folks; it's on its way.'

They watched the screen as it mimicked the virus's path across the satellite links and into the spy satellite. As soon as it was uploaded, the computer shrieked a warning and the outer layer of the virus flashed red a couple of times and disappeared.

'Ed, they've killed level one already!'

'I know, I know,' said Edison, who had sat upright in his chair and was typing furiously. He was attempting to find the commands that would get the satellite to alter its camera view toward the cell location on the south coast but as yet had failed to get it right. Another alarm rang on the computer; the second virus layer had failed.

'They're through the next layer, Ed!'

'Quick!' said Ali.

'I'm going just as quickly as I can,' replied Edison through gritted teeth.

Finally getting the correct commands, Edison spun the satellite's powerful camera into position. On a second monitor screen, another outline map of Britain appeared. Edison entered the identifying code for the south coast phone cell. The map zoomed in, adding multiple layers of detail such as major roads and building estates but it was still too far out.

'We need it closer!' demanded Ali. Edison didn't answer but felt that an exaggerated expulsion of breath would be enough.

Yet another alarm sounded through Edison's computer speakers as the third protection layer fell to the counter hacking of the government's systems.

'Ed! Only two left!' shrieked Jimmy.

Edison had given up on replying, it took too much time. Having found the program on the phone company's system that would start the triangulation calculation, Edison typed in Crackpot's mobile phone number and hit the "Locate" button on the screen. Everyone in the room watched, hardly daring to breathe as the computer paused whilst it considered the command. Then, a message appeared:

> "Phone number not active on the network, please try another"

'No!' cried Ali. 'What's going on?'

Edison rubbed his temples as he strained to find a reason for this. As he did so, his computer wailed at him again.

'Woops,' said Jimmy, 'the fourth layer's gone. You're down to the last one, Ed!'

Edison almost shouted in frustration.

'Jimmy, pass me your phone!' he said suddenly.

'What for?' replied Jimmy as he tossed the phone across to Edison.

'Because for some reason, Crackpot's mobile has dropped off the network, I'm going to send him a text message in a hope that it will bring the link back up.'

Edison's fingers darted over the miniature keypad as he typed in a message. The task completed, he threw the phone onto the desk and returned to the keyboard.

'Now come on...' he muttered to himself and retyped Crackpot's phone number into the Skittish Telecon's triangulation program. As he hit the "Locate" button once more, he saw on his monitor that the last layer of virus protection was flashing red as it came under sustained attack from the government computers. Any moment now, they would be completely visible as the spy satellite retraced Edison's entire connection through the Skittish Telecon's satellite and through the internet to his very home.

A beep from the computer made everyone jump – there was a new message on the screen:

```
"Active session for this number detected,
          triangulation complete!"
```

All eyes snapped to Edison's other monitor; the map showing the south coast had suddenly zoomed all the way in to a large abandoned warehouse by the sea. Although they could not see inside the building, there was no mistaking Crackpot's battered old estate car parked haphazardly across the pavement outside.

'We've got him!' screamed Ali.

The computer then sounded its loudest alarm yet as the final layer of virus failed completely.

'No! They're tracing us!' said Edison as he stared at the defeated virus program.

Nobody could move, they were frozen as the horror of the situation unfolded before their eyes. Everyone except Perry that is, who was shuffling so much on his makeshift stool of printer paper boxes that with an almighty crash, he pitched backwards into a heap of A4 and wires.

On a screen a new message appeared:

```
"Internet connection lost, press any key to
          attempt reconnection..."
```

As Perry rose from the pile of computer related debris, he held the internet lead in his hand, which he had just yanked from the wall socket.

'Err, sorry – have I done something bad?'

Edison looked over at the spy satellite screen, it too was displaying a message:

```
"Trace failed, connection to remote host
                terminated"
```

'That'll do nicely!' he said, beaming.

> The engine compartment of a spaceship, the south coast of England

Crackpot moaned and groaned to himself as he fiddled with connectors and miles of cables into which he was attempting to connect the small metallic device. His spine ached so much from bending into the hatch that he'd considered growing himself a new one.

As he rummaged down below, a new noise came from his mobile phone. It wasn't the first time – it had been doing it for the last twenty minutes but he'd ignored it so far but enough was enough. Reaching up and into his pocket, he grabbed the phone and pulled it back down to where his head was buried. He opened the message that was flashing on the screen.

'What what? What it mean?' he said as he read the text. 'What mean "stick your head up"?'

Crackpot decided to do just that and removed his head from the hatchway.

'If you even blink, Crackpot,' growled a female voice from behind him, 'I'm going to vaporise something off that *won't* grow back!'

Going in Alone

> The captain's quarters, Repugnatron Battle Cruiser, just past Jupiter

'FRAGNUT!' bellowed Gragnash down the ship's intercom that was cunningly disguised as a dirty-looking hosepipe. 'Get here now!'

Gragnash was sitting at his own private dining trough, before him was his long awaited supper; he was jabbing it with his cutlery in disgust.

'What in the Septic Stink-marshes of Diarrhoema Minor is *this*?' he said as Fragnut floated in on his hover trolley.

'It's your supper, almighty overlord, sir,' replied Fragnut, wringing his slimy hands together nervously.

'I know what it's supposed to be but what *is* it?' he demanded, jabbing Fragnut with his spoon.

'It's Cream of Primordial Soup, sir.'

'It's Phlegm of Unusual Poop, more like! Get me the chef, now!'

'But...sir...there is no-'

'NOW!'

Fragnut hovered over to Gragnash's intercom. 'Erm, may I...'

Gragnash waved a suitably ill-tempered reply to the affirmative. Lifting the pipe-like device, Fragnut addressed the kitchens.

'Can the...err...chef please come to the supreme overlord's quarters immediately!'

There followed a particularly uneasy silence as the captain and his Lieutenant waited for the preparer of the soup to travel up five hundred floors. Fragnut thought he'd fill the time by whistling a happy tune, only on finding that his Repugnatron physiology was nowhere near advanced enough to make such a noise he gave up, having sprayed a pool of spittle over the floor.

'Ah, Bonemangle,' said the Lieutenant as the stand-in chef finally made it through the door. 'Gragnash, almighty overlord, captain of captains, leader of lead-'

'Oh, can it, Fragnut,' interrupted Gragnash. 'Bonemangle is it? From what mangy mud mire did you shovel this filth?' he said, pointing at the bowl of soup.

'Well...sir...ahem, that'll be outa' a tin, sir,' stammered Bonemangle, who then held out his unusually small and dextrous hand to show Gragnash the tin. Gragnash slid over and snatched it.

'It's a thousand years out of date!'

109

'Ah, well, yes, but it was all I could find at the back of the cupboard, almighty overlord-'

'SILENCE! Fragnut, the trapdoor!'

'But sir-' protested Fragnut.

'Now!'

'But he's the only one that can work the-'

'NOW!'

Fragnut pulled a lever that rose prominently from the floor by Gragnash's trough. Below Bonemangle, the floor fell open and a deep, dark drop that lead directly to the Grate-O-Matic presented itself.

Nothing happened.

'Erm, Bonemangle,' said Fragnut.

'Sir?'

'Would you be so kind as to turn off your hover trolley?'

'Oh! Certainly, sir!'

Bonemangle flicked the lever by his side and, just a few seconds too late, realised exactly what he'd done. The screams of his descent were cut off by Gragnash closing the trapdoors in his wake.

'Now, Lieutenant, what news?'

'Sir? What of, sir?'

Gragnash shrugged. 'Anything,' he replied.

'Oh, okay,' said Fragnut, 'let me see, urm, ah – we seem to have lost all the chefs somewhere. They're missing presumed dead.'

'Really?' said Gragnash with surprise, 'well, if they turn up, kill them as punishment. Next.'

'Right. Okay. Got that. Kill dead chefs. Check. Next...urm...oh, due to the latter, the only things to eat come from tins.'

'That's okay, isn't it?'

'Well, sir, it would be had you not just grated the only Repugnatron capable of using a tin opener...'

'By the Inflamed Bedsores of Itchybum Major, damn it!'

'Indeed, sir.'

'Never mind, we'll be at that scrummy planet Earth soon and we'll be able to top up our Birthing pool and grow us some more chefs. How long now?'

'At the rate we're going, sir, just five hours.'

A cruel gleam flashed across Gragnash's four eyes.

'Excellent!   FIRE UP THE DESINTEGRATOR!' shouted Gragnash as if addressing a huge audience.

'But almighty overlord, you know how vulnerable we are when it's fully open!'

'Oh, Lieutenant, you always were the worrier. Open it up; we'll do a little basking on asteroids as we coast in!'

'As you wish, sir,' said Fragnut, who hovered out of the room backwards whilst bowing.

At the front of the Repugnatron Battle Cruiser, a round hatchway the size of Africa opened.   Encircling this hatchway deep rings of gigantic, rotating teeth started to appear on the inside, one on top of the other, each bigger than the last and growing outward before the ship like the biggest funnel in the universe.

> GPOL Recon craft, rooftop of an abandoned warehouse, south coast of England

111

'Tell me where you got it, Crackpot!' demanded Ali, who was in serious danger of having to reach down Crackpot's throat and retrieve the metallic object he'd been fitting to his ship once she had thrust it down there.

'Be relaxing yourself, girly,' said Crackpot, looking worried. 'Only air-freshener!'

They were in a purpose built interrogation room that seemed to have no right fitting inside the craft at all. There was a single white chair in the centre and it was to this that Crackpot was manacled by electronic means. Edison and Jimmy stood to one side, staying out of the way.

'Don't try your ridiculous bluffs on me, perpetrator; I've scanned it and it's no such thing!'

'It's not? Oopsy, Crackpot fooled...'

Ali grabbed one of the chair's arms and spun it around with all her strength. Crackpot made hi-pitched gurgling noises through his oscillating lips as he turned into an alien spinning-top.

'There's no moving parts in that chair, Crackpot,' said Ali, 'no friction to slow you down. You could be spinning there for hours!'

Crackpot made noises that sounded suspiciously like heaving.

'Ooooo...ooo...dddinner...cccoming...back...'

Ali thrust out an arm and stopped the chair. Crackpot looked decidedly green. Also in the interrogation room were Jimmy and Edison, who stood alongside Ali.

'What is it for?' said Edison, glancing at Ali.

'This,' she said, not looking back at Edison but brandishing the device at a rather poorly looking Crackpot, 'is an anti-GPOL SecurDock device. Its purpose is to get around the lock that GPOL applied to his spaceship in order to stop him sneaking off the planet without permission!'

'Really?' said Edison with interest. 'Why were you leaving in such a hurry, Crackpot? Had a tip-off that there was some unpleasantness on its way?'

'Nopey! Me know nothing about unpleasantness, me just going holiday!'

'Pull the other one, Crackpot,' said Jimmy, 'it's got bells on it!'

Those not indigenous to Earth turned and stared at him in bewilderment.

'Okay,' said Ali, turning back to Crackpot, 'if you won't tell me where you got it then I will tell you. This could only have come from one source, a source that conveniently enough we happened to meet at your house, Crackpot – the Technoids!'

'Nopey wrong; not seen Technoids, not done no business, me make air freshener!'

Ali turned the object over in her hand and put it just under Crackpot's nose.

'Humm, nicey pine fresh!'

'Can you see that, Crackpot?' she said, ignoring him and pointing to a small inscription.

'Erm, excusey pardon, me not got my glasses on...'

'Well, let me help you out here – it reads "Copyright Technoid Technologies". *Understandee*, Crackpot?'

A guilty smile spread the length of Crackpots extra wide mouth; if the electronic restraint chair he was sitting on had not blocked out the signals between his brain and his hands, he'd be drumming his purple fingernails guiltily also.

'Me talkey no more, first see lawyer!'

'No talkey? We'll see. Perry, bring the Memory Cap in.'

Perry's face suddenly appeared on a screen where a blank wall used to be.

'The Memory Cap? Are you sure?' he said. Ali gave him a look that he'd seen once too often. 'You're sure.'

He disappeared from the screen. A few moments later he entered the interrogation room with a device that looked like a long-legged, small-bodied, big-footed plastic spider.

'What's that?' said Jimmy, looking slightly unnerved at the thought of being stuck in the same room as some weird space arachnid.

'Crackpot will tell you, won't you, Crackpot?' said Ali, walking toward him having taken the object from Perry.

'Nopey no! Can't use, can't use! No right!'

'It's a brain scanner; it allows us to copy or remove thoughts, memories or even entire emotions and its going to tell us exactly what Crackpot's been up to lately. Sit still now,' said Ali, placing the device carefully on the floor, 'you wouldn't want me to accidentally wipe out your entire childhood, would you...'

Crackpot stared at it with an expression of terror. With a scrabbling of 'legs', the contraption rose and clack-clacked across the floor, climbing up his frozen body on its way to his head. Crackpot began straining in his seat, attempting to duck out of the way as it climbed higher. Just as it was about to make contact with his skull, the view screen on the wall sprang into life once more but this time it was the Admiral's tired face that filled it.

'Ah, officers, I see you've managed to apprehend Crackpot at last. Good work; bring him in immediately. Oh, cripes - are those two humans?' he added.

'Yes, sir,' said Ali.

The admiral's face seemed to age ten years in a few seconds.

'Best eject them and leave before it's too late.'

'But-'

'Officer,' interrupted the Admiral, his expression was initially stern but softened so slightly that it was almost undetectable, 'don't get involved. Safety first at all times.'

'Sir,' replied Ali through tight lips.

'Oh, and another thing,' said the Admiral, 'I hope you're not going to perform a memory scan on a suspect that has not been officially charged with a gBay related crime, are you? Please say you're not.'

'No, sir. Just a bluff, sir,' replied Ali but her face told a different story.

'Thank goodness. Then I'll expect your prisoner in the cells within the next hour, officer.'

The screen went blank and promptly vanished.

'He's all heart, your boss,' said Edison.

'Lock down,' said Ali to the ships computer, reluctantly lifting the Memory Cap from Crackpot. At this command, a translucent box of energy sprang up all around the chair in which Crackpot was secured. From within the floor rose a bed that made a bathtub full of bricks look comfortable. As it appeared, Crackpot's chair retreated into the floor, leaving him in a pile where it had once stood. Ali waved a warning finger at him, scowling.

'I haven't finished with you yet, Crackpot!' she growled. Turning, she stalked out of the room, closely followed by Jimmy and Edison.

'You can't leavey go!' cried Crackpot.

'Watch me,' said Ali and she sealed the door behind her with the resounding clang of a thick iron door. Of course, the door was not made of iron and its closing was actually silent but the ship's computer was instructed to add the sound effect in order to instil a rising sense of panic in the prisoner. It worked.

'What now?' said Edison.

'You heard,' said Ali, 'we kick you out and take our prisoner back.'

'Fine,' said Edison flippantly, 'only, you do owe me.'

'Meaning?'

'Meaning that I don't think that you really want to drop us off just so we can get mashed into a pulp and recycled.'

'You got any better ideas?'

Edison thought for a moment.

116

'Do you know where the Repugnatron ship is right now?'

'Perry?' said Ali.

Perry manipulated the controls below the view screens and a map of the solar system appeared. On it flashed a representation of the Repugnatron's ship, which was just clear of Jupiter.

'There,' he said, pointing to the screen.

'How long until they get to Earth?' asked Edison.

Perry clicked a few buttons. 'Around five hours from now.'

'Do we have to pass them to get your prisoner back?'

'We? It's *we* is it now?' said Ali.

'Well that depends on how you feel about saving an entire race of innocent beings.'

'Don't lay a guilt trip on me!' said Ali angrily.

'You feel guilty now? Just wait five hours...'

Ali stared at Edison with her dark eyes and for a while said nothing.

'What are you suggesting?'

'I need you to tell me everything you know about the Repugnatrons.'

'Why do I not like the sound of this?' said Ali, giving him a suspicious look.

Edison turned to Jimmy, his mischievous smile that meant he was up to something was upon his face.

'You ready for a scouting mission?'

'Are you joking? Where do I sign?' beamed Jimmy.

'Wait. Just wait,' said Ali, 'a scouting mission for *what*?'

Twenty minutes later Edison had absorbed just about as much information on the Repugnatrons as he felt he had time for. As he and Ali sat at a desk in an operations room skipping through some last minute data, Jimmy and Perry were searching through storage containers in the hold for a few items that Edison had requested.

'One thing has got me wondering, Perry.'

'What's that?' said Perry as he pulled two spare GPOL suits from a locker.

'How is it that you and Ali are, like, out here, doing a proper job when you're only our age – shouldn't you be at space academy or something?'

Perry chuckled.

'Space academy, good one! No, we do all our learning on the SubCon.'

'The what?'

'SubCon. It's short for Subconscious Tutoring. It's great; you drop this helmet thing on that works just like the Memory Cap but without the record function, and select a subject from the computer database. The information is then blasted into your subconscious in a few short seconds and that's it!'

'No way! You mean school's over in a few seconds?'

'Yeh,' said Perry. 'The information is supposed to filter through into your conscious memory over time. It's cool; you can go to bed and wake up the next day knowing how to strip down and rebuild sub atomic particle accelerators!'

'In theory,' said Ali, who had appeared at the door with Edison. 'But what you forgot to mention is

118

that unless you are some sort of genius, it takes weeks to assimilate such information – if at all, which rules *you* out.'

Perry pulled a face.

'How're we doing, Jimmy?' said Edison. 'Got everything?'

'Yep!'

'Good; let's get ready, time's running out.'

All four sat around the operations table, the requested kit was laid out on its surface.

'Right,' said Edison, looking serious. 'This is the plan. Jimmy and I are going to disguise ourselves as GPOL officers and are going to get you to fly us to the Repugnatron Battle Cruiser, where we will dock.'

'Can't we just beam aboard?' said Jimmy, looking crestfallen.

'No,' said Ali. 'Firstly matter transportation has been banned for biological entities since the whole Gruber twins incident – don't ask,' she added, seeing Jimmy's face, 'arms, legs and lawsuits everywhere. The only thing you can use MatTran for now is inanimate objects.'

'Like the hologram thing you beamed into my room the first day we met?' asked Edison.

'You mean the HolTran device that your house creature swallowed,' said Ali, giving Edison a most unimpressed glare. 'Yes; the HolTran allows you to project yourself anywhere as if you're really there, you really can't tell the difference by looking. The only problem is that you can't touch or interact with anything other than the HolTran projector itself, which has its own anti-gravity generators and will move

119

around as if you're actually touching it. Useful if you want to go walkies.'

'That's a shame,' said Jimmy, 'I was looking forward to being beamed up.'

'Really?' said Ali, 'you were looking forward to having a laser-beam slice through every molecule of your body, making a note of exactly where that molecule lives, writing it down in an A to Z map of You, running it through a compression algorithm to make your trip quicker, and destroying you where you stand in the hope that there will be not so much as a flicker of power loss on the other side when you are being rebuilt bit by tiny little bit? Rather you than me...'

'Right,' said Edison after a moment of contemplation by the group, 'MatTran and HolTran are both out anyway.'

'Why?' said Perry.

'Because according to your computer files, the Repugnatron ship has been fitted with transport beam inhibitors, the only place you can actually beam anything into is the escape pods, and these are secured to stop access into the ship so that's that.

'So, when we dock, I will go aboard the Repugnatron ship leaving Jimmy here until called. I will then attempt to stop their ship from travelling any further until we have gathered enough information to come up with a final plan. During all this, you two keep out of sight,' he added, looking at the two GPOL officers. Ali looked scandalized.

'Why do *we* have to hide? Why is it that you two are going aboard instead of us?'

'Firstly,' said Edison, 'you've already told me that you confronted Gragnash and his crew over the Earth sale; he's not likely to allow you in if he thinks you're going to try and stop him. Secondly, you may not be aware but you've got an attitude problem and would be throttling him within the first thirty seconds of getting aboard.'

'But-'

'No but's,' interrupted Edison, 'we go in alone.'

Ali stormed off in a huff.

'Women,' said Edison. Jimmy and Perry nodded.

A few minutes later and all four were strapped into chairs behind the control console, Edison and Jimmy's chairs having risen from within the floor to accommodate them.

'Do we really need restraint belts?' asked Jimmy nervously.

'The mood I'm in?' growled Ali. 'Yes.'

After barking her way through the pre-flight checks, she grabbed the control stick.

'Hold on!' she snapped and yanked the stick hard backwards. Edison's cheeks felt like they'd been nailed to the roof of the warehouse whilst the remainder of his head had been rocketed upward giving him instant jowls that flapped around like shopping bags in a gale. Moving his eyes toward the view screen, he saw the warehouse turn into a speck, closely followed by the coastline. Within a few seconds, the screen flashed white as they accelerated upward through a dense patch of altostratus cloud before a dome of blackness grew at the top of the screen.

Edison felt his face return back to its normal parameters as the ship decelerated having passed through Earth's upper atmosphere.

'There,' said Perry with a smile, 'your first trip into space!'

Edison and Jimmy stared with wonder at the view screen as planet Earth hung below them, a collection of instantly recognisable landmass and deep blue sea.

'Amazing,' was all Jimmy could manage as he watched the seemingly motionless planet and its complete tranquillity. From up here it was hard to believe that anything but peace and beauty prevailed on its surface.

'Finished sightseeing, humans? Then prepare for hyper-speed.'

Edison baulked at the thought of going any faster; after all, he'd only just got his face back. 'And how fast is hyper-speed, exactly?'

'Just below light speed,' replied Ali, not looking up from the console.

'How do you manage to avoid things at that speed?' said Edison with deep-rooted concern. Space may be a once in a lifetime trip but he would prefer it if it wasn't a last in a lifetime trip.

'At that speed we gain almost infinite mass so we slice through asteroids like a laser knife through butter and we don't end up burying ourselves in planet's molten cores as we know where most of them are. Most of them...'

Edison's imagination threw up terrifying images of Ali trying to steer around a moon whilst going at near light speed. Images made worse by repressed childhood memories of his mother's almost suicidal negotiations of traffic islands in her Ford Cortina.

'You scared, human?' said Ali, smirking as she rotated the ship to face away from the Earth.

'Me? Nah,' said Edison with a far too casual shrug. 'I've been in scarier lifts than this.'

Ali looked over her shoulder at Edison; she had a dangerous gleam in her eye.

'Ding ding, going up! Scream when it's your floor!'

'I don't screa-'

At that moment, Ali slammed her finger down on a pulsating red button. On the view screen, the pinpricks of starlight smeared themselves into lines as a firestorm of electric blue exploded across the display and movement within the cabin seemed to pause and shudder as time momentarily fell over itself. Inside all was quiet, apart from Edison, whose scream lasted almost the entire thirty-two second journey to the outskirts of Jupiter.

The deceleration from near light speed to an almost snail pace of one hundred thousand miles per hour technically had no physical effects on the ships occupants, although try telling that to Edison, who felt like he'd just slammed a powerboat into the side of HMS Totallyunmovable. When he'd managed to retake control of his eyes, Edison looked over at Jimmy who, with his chest heaving, was predictably smiling. Although to be fair, he was staring wide-eyed ahead. As Edison watched, Jimmy's hand inched ever higher from where it had been gripping the chair. Bit by bit it rose until it came to an eventual stop. Without any change in expression the hand moved, the fingers pulled into a fist and so slowly that you'd almost need a time-lapse camera to film the event, a thumb came out and stuck itself up in the air. This was the clincher – Jimmy was more than just okay.

It took a few moments longer before they both regained full use of their mental and physical states. Perry and Jimmy appeared to be having their own personal grinning competition whilst Edison tried to make up for his embarrassing lack of composure by manoeuvring himself into various cool positions in his chair.

'There they are!' said Ali, who was pointing to a vast, round gap where the stars should have been.

'What am I looking at?' said Edison, who was standing before the view screen with Ali.

'Enhance the picture, Perry,' said Ali.

Perry typed a few commands into the console and the image sharpened, causing horrifying detail to appear. They watched as the picture showed thousands of rings of enormous metallic teeth rotating in opposing directions within a funnel, the proportions of which would be totally unfathomable to most Earthlings.

'Is...is that as big as it looks?' said Jimmy, who was pointing at the screen rather limply.

'Bigger,' said Perry.

'Big enough to engulf your planet,' said Ali. Jimmy made a noise like air escaping from a punctured tyre.

'Then we'd better get onboard and buy us some time,' said Edison, looking resolute once more. 'Officer, make contact.'

'Are you sure about this?' said Ali.

'Entirely.'

Perry returned to the ship's controls again, adjusting the view area of the onboard cameras so that he and Ali would not be seen by the Repugnatrons. When done, a communications screen appeared on the viewer. They waited for the call to be answered.

When eventually the Repugnatrons did answer, Edison could not help but recoil at the sight of Fragnut's face, which reminded him of a brown, lumpy toad with far too many eyes. It was a face that he swore would put him off his food for at least a week.

'This is the Repugnatron Battle Cruiser of the almighty overlord, Gragnash. Speak now or we will "accidentally" suck you into our Disintegrator!'

'This is officer GP234 of GPOL, Milky Way sector,' said Edison, using his best casual voice. 'We are carrying out routine safety checks and demand that you let us aboard your ship.'

Fragnut laughed, causing Edison to think that the Lieutenant was having a major pulmonary seizure.

'What, do you think I'm stupid? You can't fool me; you've got no right to come aboard our ship!'

'But we have reason to believe that your quantum flux capacitor is leaking super ionised atomic warp fluid all over your double sprocketed exhaust manifold. That's a fire hazard, don't you know?'

'Oh,' said Fragnut, fire was one of the few things that Repugnatron's *did* understand. 'Then you'd better come on over.'

The screen went dead.

'You heard the dung,' said Edison. 'Take us in, officer.'

With a burst of acceleration, Ali sent the ship in a monumental arc that would take them to the dark side of the Battle Cruiser, to the docking hatch and right into the clutches of the Repugnatrons.

Missing In Action

No sooner had the electro-magnetic docking clamps secured the GPOL ship to the battle cruiser then Edison had unbuckled himself from his seat and was making for the access platform at the centre of the craft. He was already wearing one of the spare GPOL suits, which had automatically adjusted its size to fit him. Around his waist sat a utility belt that was missing a standard issue Vaporiser.

'Are you sure you don't want to arm yourself?' said Ali. 'I know it'd contravene a million GPOL laws, but under the circumstances...'

'No, I don't trust myself not to vaporise my legs by accident.'

'If you're sure, but I don't like it,' she said, scowling.

'Now, now, Ali. Any more of that and I will start thinking you care.'

Ali rose from her seat and walked over to where he stood. Placing a hand on either side of his head, she pulled it forward gently.

'Err…Ali…don't be getting all sentimental on me,' stammered Edison, who in a rare moment was caught off guard. Ali looked at him, smiled, and then thrust what felt like a dustbin into each ear.

'Ouch!' cried Edison, who'd been yanked out of his soft-focus moment. 'What've you done?'

'Relax, they're only micro translators. Without them you'd be hearing the Repugnatrons as they actually sound and believe me, you don't want that.'

'Well, I'm eternally grateful,' muttered Edison, grimacing.

'My pleasure!' replied Ali. Edison thought this was probably true.

'Remember, Jimmy, don't come till I call,' he said, shaking his head like a dog dislodging water from its ears.

'Roger!' said Jimmy, saluting.

'Okay, Perry, let me down.'

Perry pressed a few virtual buttons on the control panel and the access platform started to sink.

'Oh, Ed – don't forget this,' said Jimmy, throwing a clipboard and pen into the hole in the centre of the ship. The clipboard had been taken from Jimmy's school bag and had, until a few moments ago, had his homework pinned to it: "A Public Questionnaire on the Grooming Habits of the Over Sixties". Needless to say, it was still waiting to be done.

'Ooof! Thanks,' said Edison as it whacked him on the head.

The platform stopped at the bottom of what looked like the inside of a major sewer pipe. There was no obvious lighting but there was a menacing green hue to everything, a glow that was enough for you to see where you were going – not that seeing where you were going was comforting in any way.

With a sigh of resignation, Edison stepped from the access platform and into the dampness of the pipe. His foot splashed before crunching on something - he had no interest in finding out what.

There was no way to go other than forward so Edison did just that, walking along the pipe making loud splashing and crunching noises as he went. He was sure that he would be met at some point soon; if the noise his feet were making didn't attract attention then the sound of his moaning would. As he suspected, he'd only walked a few hundred metres when a pile of something floated toward him on a hover trolley.

'Oy! You! GPOL. Follow me an' keep up,' said the Repugnatron on meet-and-greet duties.

'Nice to meet you too,' said Edison.

'Dun' go getting cute or I'll do for ya'.'

The Repugnatron waved a club at Edison menacingly.

'So, where are you taking me?'

'Bridge. Almighty overlord wants to check ya' out.'

This news pleased Edison; it had been his plan to get to the bridge from the start.

They had been moving through the tunnels for nearly ten minutes. Edison had been trying to memorise the various junctions that they took not only so that he could find his way back out, but so he could relay them to Jimmy.

Then Edison saw a glow of yellowy light coming from a little further up the corridor on the right. The closer they got, the clearer it became until they finally pulled level with it. The Repugnatron slid straight past, paying it no attention but Edison stopped and peered in through a window set into an impenetrable looking door. It was Edison's guess that he was looking at a prison cell of some kind. This was evident from not only the sparse interior and the feeding hatch set into the door but also the five creatures that were huddled together in a dark corner, creatures that certainly were not Repugnatrons.

'Oy! Come on, nearly there,' said the guard, who managed to sound out of breath despite having only to hover on his trolley. 'No angin' around; I've got a group boil-scratchin' session t' go to.'

Edison followed, walking away from the cell and the thought of a Repugnatron boil-scratching session.
A short trudge further on and Edison was lead through a hole just vacated by what looked like a sliding toilet lid and onto the bridge of the battle cruiser. Edison stopped for a moment and took it in; the place was like a huge, interstellar railway signal box. As he looked around, he was filled with a feeling of utter revulsion.

A prod between the shoulder blades sent him stumbling forward a couple of steps.

'Well, well, well. If it isn't our little GPOL Safety Champion. Breed 'em small, don't they at your place.'

It was Gragnash, his Lieutenant was smirking just behind him. Edison handed over one of his best sneers. It was accepted without comment.

'Still, we're all *very* pleased to eat you!'

Didn't he mean *meet you?* thought Edison. He cursed Ali and her dustbin ear-translators. Discrepancies like this could really change the course of your day.

'As am I,' he lied - well, start as you mean to go on and all that. He brandished his clipboard, licked the nib of his pen and scribbled something onto the paper.

Edison had a theory. It was a new theory and basically it went something like this: "I don't care how advanced your life-form, when someone comes poking around their spaceship with a clipboard and pen, they're going to start sweating."

And so it was.

Gragnash looked like he'd just swallowed a vat of chilli peppers on a rather hot day.

'Is...err...everything okay?' he said, attempting to peek over Edison's shoulder as he studied every inch of the bridge and made notes.

'Sir. *Please*. This is a delicate business. A mere blink and I could miss a Quatermass Instability Vortex in your upper left quadrant...'

Despite the theoretical odds on him pulling it off, Gragnash managed to successfully fuse together in perfect harmony a groan, a whimper and gulp.

Edison's pen skipped over the paper. Unfortunately, because all GPOL video stream recorders were built into the helmet, which Edison wasn't allowed to wear on the Repugnatron bridge, he had no official way of recording what he was looking at.

But then, how often did Edison play by the official rules?

'Gragnash,' said Edison, tapping his pen onto his paper in a considering way. Fragnut was over to him in a second with what the Lieutenant had designed to be a snarl on his face.

'That's Supreme Overlo-'

'Lieutenant Fragnut, calm down,' said a nervous looking Gragnash. 'We don't want to be missing one of those, erm, Craterpants Invisibility Gortex, things, do we GPOL, eh?'

'Exactly,' affirmed Edison. 'Now, what type of Neutrino Concentrator do you have?'

Gragnash and Fragnut looked at each other like someone had just said: "Nineteen down, six letters, *to be two sandwiches short of one of these*". In their defence though, they did seem to be making all the right noises associated with trying to work it out. Eventually, however, they gave up. It's the Repugnatron way. If it had been an object and not a question, they'd have walloped it with a club.

'No idea,' said Fragnut.

Good, thought Edison.

'Damn,' said Edison. 'Never mind, if you just turn it on and, say, bring up the last thing you bought using it then it will give off enough, erm, Super Saturated Microwaves for me to see if it's faulty.'

'Right away,' said Gragnash, who was getting nervous at being reminded that there was actually horrid technology hiding underneath all these lovely levers and pulleys. 'Lieutenant, make it-'

'"*So*"?' offered Edison.

'Work,' finished Gragnash. Edison groaned - what a gulf in class.

Fragnut hovered over to a bank of levers that were unremarkable from all the thousands of others. Edison watched like a hawk. After sliding past a few more, Fragnut stopped and positioned himself between the levers and Edison, who cursed to himself. He had hoped to get some clue as to how the system worked — just in case, but it would've been useless anyway. Even if he'd had an unobstructed view, Fragnut's hands whirred over the console just as quickly as Edison's hands over his own keyboards.

'All done!' said Fragnut, who was pointing up to the eye-like screen and what his gBay account stated was his last purchase.

Edison raised a single eyebrow.

'Lieutenant?' said Gragnash.

'Sir?'

'Does your standard issue chafe your sensitive skin?'

Fragnut looked up. There, emblazoned across the centre of the screen in sixty million mega pixels, was a picture of a big, pink, love-heart pillow, replete with fury pink edging and a message in the middle saying: "I love Uranus!"

Fragnut moved so fast he almost left his trolley behind. Grabbing a bunch of levers, he cleared the screen.

'Maybe the item *before* that would do?' offered Edison. Fragnut mumbled something about sensitive skin as he fiddled with the system again.

Bingo, thought Edison as the sales page for Earth appeared.

'Okay, that'll do,' he said, sounding deliberately uninterested in the item on the screen. 'If you would be so kind to step, err, hover, to one side, I'd like to take a reading if I may.'

Fragnut did so; he wasn't at all keen on getting super saturated by microwaves. From within a pouch on his belt, Edison took out a small silver object and flipped it open, pointing it at the console and screen.

'Urgurh,' said Gragnash in discomfort at seeing blatant techno-wizardry without the usual veil of cold, hard iron. 'What's *that*?'

'Oh, it's just a Super Saturated Microwave Leakage detector,' said Edison casually. In fact it was his mobile phone and he was now pointing the inbuilt camera lens at the screen and console whilst using the video capture option to record as much information about the scene as possible.

'How're we looking?' said Gragnash nervously, who was beginning to leave large pools of what Edison hoped was sweat on the floor below his hover trolley.

'Well,' said Edison, he had finished his recording of all the information he needed and was ready to kick in the next stage of his delaying plan, 'unless my detector makes a horrendous noise, everything's okay.'

Without retracting the phone from the direction of the console, Edison cancelled the video recording function and switched to the built-in MP3 player.

Skipping down the albums, he selected a track by *The Cheeky Girls*. As a snippet of track played out of the phone's small speaker, the Repugnatrons seemed to go into abject distress.

'Nooooo! Please make it stop!'

Edison clicked the pause button. 'It has that effect on most people,' he mumbled.

'W...w...what?' stuttered a suitably shaken Fragnut.

'I said: that's the horrible noise I was talking about. It seems you have a problem with your Neutrino Concentrator. I must take a look straight away or the results could be catastrophic!'

'Yes...yes...carry on,' whimpered Gragnash.

Edison knelt down so that he was facing the steel panels below the console. Each one was thick enough to take an assault by an angry Repugnatron but was kept in place by a screw in each corner. There was also a round disk in the centre which, when spun around with a finger, revealed what looked like a socket of some sort but Edison wasn't interested in this, just in getting the panel off.

Reaching into his pouch again, he pulled out one of the devices that Perry had found in the GPOL stores. It was a screwdriver the like of which you were never going to find in your local hardware store. It had a single button on the handle and the end of the shaft was smooth. When you placed the end against one of the millions of different screw heads found throughout the galaxy, it moulded and secured itself to the screw at the touch of the button and not even a Repugnatron temper tantrum was going to get it off.

Within a few moments, Edison had undone all of the screws and had pulled the panel forward a few centimetres.

'I'm now going to remove the panel,' declared Edison. Gragnash and Fragnut whimpered at the thought: naked technology - urk!

Edison pulled the top of the panel forward until it lay on the floor - there were whimpers and even an audible sob from the audience. The inside was a mass of what looked like transparent pipes full of water, tying themselves in knots around a Neutrino concentrator.

'Ah, just as I thought,' said Edison, who had poked his head in closer in a display of fearlessness, or so the Repugnatrons thought. 'You've an old version, an AstroUplink Two Thousand. You know, it's a wonder it hasn't burnt your bridges for you already.'

'But we only have one bridge,' said Fragnut with a frown.

'Yes, but it'll burn all the same. Now listen very carefully, I will say this only once.' Gragnash and Fragnut grimaced in an impressive display of concentration. Impressive to another Repugnatron that is; it simply made Edison's skin crawl. 'Your AstroLink's connected to your googolplex controller. Your googolplex controller's connected to your gravitational hoist singularity. Your gravitational hoist singularity's connected to your turbine anti-jitter idle valve. Your turbine anti-jitter idle valve's connected to your plasma warp drive and your plasma warp drive's attached to your fuel tanks.'

'Huh?' said both Repugnatrons.

'Okay, I'll cut a long story short: your AstroLink neutrino concentrator is connected into your fuel tanks and could overheat them, causing a cataclysmic explosion.'

'Oh,' said Gragnash, 'that I do understand.'

'Good, so you'll also understand that we have to shut down the engines on this ship immediately!'

'Hey, now wait a minute, GPOL midget,' said Fragnut, 'we're not stopping for anyone!'

'True,' said Edison. 'When those tanks go off, you'll all be turned into microscopic bio-matter and will be propelled in an outward direction from the centre of your exploding spaceship. I doubt that you'll stop for light-years.'

Fragnut and Gragnash exchanged worried looks. This was what Edison had been waiting for, this was the bait writhing on the hook.

'But that's your choice,' he continued. 'Explode now, explode a little later. Whatever floats your anti-grav chamber. I'll just be off before it's too late...'

Edison made to move back toward the exit.

'Now, err, let's not be too hasty,' said Gragnash. 'isn't there anything we can do? How about if I hit it with my club?'

'Ah, no. You can't do that,' said Edison.

'And why not?' said Fragnut, his hands on his - well, where hips would normally be on a person.

'Because,' said Edison, after a long sigh, 'the old AstroLink models were filled with highly concentrated anti-matter farmed from the event horizon of decaying stars. If you were to compromise the stability of the container, it would leak antimatter into your spaceship and the whole thing would simply blink out of existence.'

'What,' said Gragnash, 'just – poof! Gone?'

'Poof,' confirmed Edison.

'But there must be something that can be done about it, surely?' said Gragnash.

'Well, a Thermal Spike Regulator would do the trick but it'll take two months to get one ordered up, supplied *and* fitted.'

'What!' gasped Fragnut. 'Two months! We haven't got two months, we're on important business.'

'Ain't there nothing you can do, GPOL?' pleaded Gragnash. Edison rubbed his chin thoughtfully.

'Well…I could…but no, I couldn't…'

'Yes, yes you could!' said Gragnash. 'Could what?'

'Well,' said Edison, hesitantly, 'I have got a Thermal Spike Regulator back on my ship…you could have it but you'd have to fit it yourselves. It's simple enough, but we are not allowed to do this as it's normally done by our installation team; I'm sure you can understand.'

'Yes! Of course!' said Gragnash. 'Go fetch it!'

'No need, I'll have my colleague bring it onboard,' said Edison and he accessed his wrist computer, making the Repugnatrons positively yelp with fear as the three dimensional icons projected themselves into the air.

'Officer GP235, are you receiving me?' he said when he had opened a communications link back to the GPOL spaceship.

'Affirmative,' replied Jimmy, sounding relieved to hear signs of life from his friend at last.

'Officer, can you bring the spare Thermal Spike Regulator to the Repugnatron Bridge? Directions to follow.'

'Affirmative. Thermal Spike Regulator.'

'Don't worry about directions, GPOL,' said Gragnash, 'I'll have someone meet your partner at the docking point.'

Edison hesitated for a moment.

'Did you copy that, 235?'

'Affirmative,' said Jimmy. 'To be met at docking point.'

Edison's insides began to squirm like a bag of eels. This was the pivotal stage approaching. Make or break. But there'd be no smack on the wrist by the law and a telling off by mum if this one went awry; if this one went pear-shaped, he was alone and in space and no one would hear him scream...

Ali paced up and down; she didn't like this, she didn't like it at all.

'I don't like this; I don't like this at all,' she said frowning at Jimmy. 'Why you? This is a dangerous situation and a legitimate GPOL officer should be involved. Not some...some...*human*!'

Jimmy looked affronted.

'Me 'n Ed always work together - we're a team! If Ed thought this was a job for GPOL then he'd have you involved.'

He stepped onto the platform to be lowered in. 'Is anyone going to let me down?'

There was a pause before Ali spoke.

'Actually, no.'

To kill time waiting for Jimmy to arrive with the Thermal Spike Regulator, Edison made more notes on his clipboard. He was interested when strange red characters appeared on the view screen, flashing in time with a warning bell.

'There goes another one, almighty overlord, sir,' said Fragnut, pushing and pulling a few levers.

'We must get that fixed,' said Gragnash, absentmindedly.

'Trouble?' said Edison, trying to sound casual.

'No,' said Fragnut, 'it's just the emergency evacuation pods. They keep, well, falling off. Still, we've plenty.'

'Must be a big job. Maintaining a Battle Cruiser's systems I mean,' said Edison. 'A full time headache, I would imagine.'

'We've got it covered,' said Fragnut guardedly.

'Well, whatever happens you'll have to fit the Regulator yourselves – nobody else on or off this ship must know we've supplied this else you could be banned from the gBay network for good.' Fragnut gulped and muttered some more about sensitive skin.

Just when Edison was beginning to give up on Jimmy ever finding his way to the bridge, the door swung back and the same Repugnatron guard that had escorted him in was back with yet another GPOL-suited visitor.

As Edison looked over, his brow furrowed – this was not Jimmy, it was Perry. Panic started to rise within; it's little things like this that can really blow an operation wide open. Why wasn't Jimmy here? At least Perry had the package with him - must keep up appearances.

'Ah, officer GP235, thanks for that and remember: not a word.'

'Absolutely, Ed - I mean, officer GP234, your secret's safe with me!'

Edison cringed; Jimmy was a pro in these circumstances but Perry might say something that might raise suspicion.

'Haven't I seen you before?' said Gragnash, who hovered over to Perry and poked him with a slimy finger. Edison felt his blood temperature cooling rapidly.

'No, I don't think so,' he said quickly. 'Not unless we've inspected this ship before and I'm sure that's not the case.'

Perry kept quiet but was looking decidedly shifty all of a sudden.

'Hummm,' said Gragnash, eyeing Perry for some time.

'Very small and dextrous hands you have there,' said Fragnut, looking at Perry's trembling digits. 'Any good with a tin-opener?'

'Anyway, here's the Thermal Spike Regulator,' said Edison, trying to move the attention away from Perry.

Both Gragnash and Fragnut looked like the last two members left in the "How to beat your Space Tarantula phobia" class; they had simultaneously withdrawn their hands close to their chest and were breathing heavily as Edison opened the box.

'Don't worry, it won't bite,' he said, suppressing a grin and pulling out Crackpot's illegal anti-SecurDock device from the box.

'Who wants it?' he said, offering it between the two petrified looking Repugnatrons.

'Y..you take it, Lieutenant,' said Gragnash, giving Fragnut's trolley a little push.

'Oooooh, I...I don't know, sir,' said Fragnut, trying to slow the trolley down by using hand-paddles in the air.

'I've got a seniority wall chart and a gnarly club that says otherwise, Fragnut!' growled Gragnash.

Fragnut bowed to the inevitable and put out his hand. All of his eyes were quivering in their sockets. As the object fell into his grasp, he gave a high-pitched little scream. This time Edison could no more hold back his pleasure than a teabag could hold back the contents of the Hoover dam.

'Watch it, you little freakster!' stammered Fragnut.

'Right back at you, four eyes!' said Edison under his breath.

'What did you say?' said Gragnash.

'There's more in the pack but it's only for your eyes.'

'Oh.'

Edison reached into the box and pulled out a folded piece of paper, handing it over to Gragnash.

'Remember: shut the engines down first and keep this between you!' he said tapping the side of his nose; a gesture that meant about as much to a

Repugnatron as "Tossing the Kibblewot" does to a human.

Fragnut reached over and pulled a few levers; the engines powered down and the craft came to a complete halt.

'Officer GP234, our work here is done,' said Edison and grabbing Perry's elbow, he manoeuvred him to the doorway. 'Good luck!' he said, giving Gragnash and Fragnut a friendly wave but the two had unfurled the instruction sheet and were already tying themselves in knots trying to follow the steps.

'Come on, let's get out of here,' said Edison into Perry's ear and they both turned and sped off down the corridor.

It was not long before they were approaching the prison cell that Edison had looked into on the way to the bridge. Peering in through the window, he saw that the cell was now completely empty.

'What's in there?' said Perry.

'Nothing now,' replied Edison, wondering what had befallen the unfortunate occupants. 'Let's go.'

It seemed like a long way back; Edison was keeping quiet in order to remember the junctions in reverse. Eventually they saw the glow of the GPOL transport platform and ran. It was a relief to leave behind the wet, crunchy pipe floor and feel something solid underfoot again. Stepping onto the platform, it began to rise - not nearly quick enough for Edison.

Their heads were beginning to enter the ship when Perry gave a startled cry and crashed to the floor. Edison jumped back in surprise and saw a slimy hand grabbing at Perry's ankles.

'No!' he cried but it was too late, Perry was yanked from the platform, disappearing into the darkness. 'They've got him!' he shouted as the platform reached the top. 'Get this thing back down!'

Ali let out a gasp before running to the control panel.

'It's stuck!' she yelled. 'They've locked the docking bay!'

At that moment the ship's computer bellowed an audio alert.

'Proactive anti-docking procedures detected. Explosive devices set to detonate in ten...nine...eight...'

'Oops,' said Jimmy.

'Time to go!' shouted Edison.

'But Perry!'

'They're going to blow us off the side of the ship!'

'We can't leave him!'

'If we don't go now, there'll be no "we" left to come back for him!'

Ali stood frozen to the spot, at a complete loss as to what to do.

'...five...four...'

'We need to be gone,' said Jimmy.

'*Now*!' added Edison.

Ali snapped back to action. Within a second she had released the electromagnetic docking clamps that bound their ship to the Repugnatrons. 'Hold onto something!' she said and brought her hand down hard on the control stick.

'*...one!*' said the computer. As the GPOL craft detached itself from the battle cruiser, the entire

144

docking hatch ignited with a blinding explosion. Ali was powerless to stop her ship spinning out into space, the force tossing them like leaf in a storm. The internal gravity systems stopped them being thrown around and breaking bones but it didn't stop them feeling utterly sick. Eventually the ship's emergency flight control kicked in and their craft stopped spinning and bucking through space.

'Everyone okay?' groaned Edison.

'Tuesday,' said Jimmy, rubbing his forehead.

Good enough, thought Edison. 'How about you?' he said, looking over to Ali.

'Fine,' she said bitterly, looking at the shrinking Repugnatron ship on the view screen. She was attempting to make contact but was getting no response.

'We will get him back.'

'How?' said Ali, who now thumped her fist down on the console, trying to look angry but Edison could see the distress in her eyes.

'We just need to adjust our plan and add a rescue mission to it.'

'What plan?' yelled Ali. 'We haven't even got a plan!'

'I'm working on it.'

For a while nobody spoke.

'Well, what now?' said Ali, breaking the uneasy silence.

'First things first — you'd best check on your detainee.'

Ali punched at the console and Crackpot's dishevelled face appeared on the view screen. He was staggering around his containment cell like he was drunk.

'Be getting me back to base, girly. Better to take my chances in prison then with your driving.' At this point he crashed onto his backside with a groan. Ali shut off the view screen with contempt.

'It is a good place to start,' suggested Edison. 'You've got a deadline to keep anyway.'

'But-'

'Don't worry about Perry, I don't think they'd risk hurting a GPOL officer and we know *exactly* where they're heading.'

Ali was quiet for a moment; she knew it made sense but was finding it hard to make the decision to leave without her partner.

'Look,' said Edison, 'they won't let us re-dock, they won't talk to us, we know their plans. Let's just go back to your headquarters, get rid of Crackpot and examine my notes. Go from there. What do you say?'

Ali nodded limply.

'But when we come back, Gragnash is mine!' she said, a ferocious gleam in her eye.

'Be my guest,' said Edison.

With a last look at the Repugnatron battle cruiser, Ali hammered some numbers into the console. 'Buckle up; Crackpot's got one last ride to remember us by...'

With that, she put the ship through three completely needless slingshots around Jupiter before entering hyper-speed.

In his cell Crackpot got a second look at his dinner after all. It wasn't a pretty sight. But then Salamanderine food never is.

The Ex-phial

It took a good five minutes for Edison to regain his composure after they had come out of hyper-speed and even then he was in danger of completely over-compensating. Jimmy was fine; he seemed to have acclimatised to this near light-speed travel stuff and had been following Ali around the ship as she made preparations for her return to the GPOL space station.

'Where are we?' said Edison.

'I could tell you,' said Ali, 'but I'd have to kill you.' She gave Edison a humourless stare. He felt that she might be telling the truth.

Ali returned to her seat in front of the console. 'We're coming up on GPOL HQ,' she said, gesturing toward the screen before her. Edison and Jimmy appeared at her side.

'Wow!' said Jimmy. On the screen, a huge structure appeared that looked like two gigantic dinner plates, one upside down on top of the other. Each "plate" was rotating in the opposite direction to the other and there were thin shafts of green light darting out from the gap in-between.

'What're those beams all about?' asked Jimmy.

'Docking guidance.'

'This place must be really busy.'

'Oh yeah,' said Ali in an understated way.

It didn't take long before the space station loomed so large in the view screen that they could no longer make out the extremities.

'*Docking guidance initiated,*' declared the onboard computer and the entire ship was bathed in a beam of green light. In response, the control stick withdrew itself back into the console as it was no longer required – GPOL headquarters now had control of their ship for the remainder of their flight in.

'Now listen up,' said Ali. 'Let me do the talking, we're in enough trouble as it is without your smart remarks making it worse.'

Edison tutted loudly; he assumed that comment was aimed at him.

'Oh, and you'd better get out of those GPOL uniforms, quick.'

The arrivals area that Edison and Jimmy found themselves in was organised chaos. There were GPOL officers disembarking from corridors every few meters, spewing out into a vast white hall. The last time Edison had seen white this bright it was coming from the presenter's teeth on the shopping channel. Most of the other GPOL officers were leading some wretched looking creature to the cells, presumably for some gBay related offence. Edison and Jimmy goggled at all the different types of life-forms. There was a creature that looked to have a chicken's lower half with a Yeti's upper body, one that resembled a shrub from Edison's garden (it was having to be watered as it was escorted) and one that kept trying to slosh out of the bucket it was being carried in.

'If only Charles Darwin could see this,' muttered Edison.

A few yards in front of them, Ali prodded and poked a reluctant Crackpot into walking faster.

'Is this all you've got, Crackpot?' she said. 'Can't you get those stumpy little legs moving any quicker?'

'You being a fine one to talk, girly. Not so big yourself.'

'I'm big enough to throw you in a cell and throw away the key-code!' she said through gritted teeth.

'Small girly, big attitude...' This one earned him a kick up the backside.

They eventually came to one of the many holding-cell front desks.

'Next,' said an overweight looking man behind the counter without looking up. Ali pushed Crackpot forward so that he hit the counter with an 'oof!'

'Oh, hello Ali, it's been a long time. What've you got for us today?'

'WHO!' shouted Crackpot from below the console. '*Who* have you been gotting for us today!'

'Crackpot,' replied Ali, ignoring the outburst.

150

'What – *the* Crackpot from the Gallepede cluster?' said the man behind the counter with an astonished look.

'Yep, the very same.'

'What've you got him in on?'

'Selling gBay property to an unauthorised race without permission.'

'Oooh, that's a good one – a nice long break for you, Crackpot,' said the man with a wide smile. Crackpot blew him a raspberry from his hidden position, some of the spittle even made it up onto the console.

'Delta section, 4325 - take him down!' growled the man. He pressed a button on his console and from within the desk, a silver spherical object around the size of a tennis ball shot out and hovered before them.

'What's that for?' said Jimmy, staring at the device with wonder.

'Just follow it,' said Ali, who then pushed Crackpot roughly in the direction in which the silver ball had floated.

The silver ball was the GPOL equivalent of in-car satellite navigation. The idea was that it became invisible to anyone other than the arresting officers (you wouldn't want to get it confused with another one and end up in the wrong place) and would lead the party through the maze of corridors until you arrived at your allotted destination. It was thought up after a criminal spent the whole of his sentence being led around in circles trying to find his cell, only to be told when he'd eventually got there that he'd served his time and was free to go.

'Are you sure you've nothing to tell us?' said Ali as they arrived at Crackpot's cell door. Crackpot turned to Jimmy and smiled.

'Nicey good hat – want to trade?'

Ali pushed Crackpot in through the door, which sealed itself with a shimmering light.

'You just wait, Crackpot; give it a week and you'll be begging us for a deal.'

'Go practice driving, girly!'

Ali's face turned a bright shade of red. Reaching out, she prodded a red button next to the door lock.

'What was that?' enquired Edison.

'Oh, just a safety device,' she said with a faint smile.

In fact it was an emergency system designed to pacify irate prisoners by zapping them with a nerve-freezing ray. In the prison cell, Crackpot fell to the floor with a crash, rigid as a length of wood, although it didn't stop him from cursing everyone and everything within earshot.

An alert from Ali's communicator turned their attentions away from the bad language coming from Crackpot's cell. Ali pressed a button to accept the incoming call. The hazy three-dimensional figure of the Admiral appeared before them, the display making him look even more tired and harassed than normal.

'Have you brought Crackpot in?'

'Yes, sir; I was going to tell you-'

'I bet that's not all you were going to tell me, was it?' he groaned. 'Get yourselves over to my office – and bring your "accessories" with you.'

'So,' said the Admiral, popping some pills and rubbing his temples with so much pressure that he was threatening to give himself an aneurism, 'let me get this absolutely straight. Despite orders to the contrary, you did not come directly back to head quarters with your prisoner, but instead decided to call in on the Repugnatrons under the completely fictitious and illegal pretence of being-' at this point the Admiral checked some hand written notes that he'd made during Ali's confession, '- safety inspectors.'

'Yes, but-'

'Further more,' he said, gesturing toward Edison and Jimmy, who were keeping quiet in their seats, 'you allowed these unauthorised beings to wear GPOL uniforms in order for them to impersonate GPOL officers.'

'Yes, but-'

'If all this were not bad enough, you also managed to allow one of our actual officers to be detained. Have I missed anything?'

Ali's face was seething with emotion.

'You've made it quite clear that you don't care in the slightest if these humans lose their planet to the Repugnatrons, but I do! Edison saved my life and probably Perry's life too – surely that counts for something?'

'Please listen, Alianna; humans are a selfish, dangerous breed who know only how to bring about misery and destruction upon themselves and all other life forms. They were probably trying to save their own

153

miserable skins when they inadvertently saved yours too. If they weren't about to be wiped off the face of the universe, GPOL would still have nothing to do with them.'

'Don't mind me,' muttered Edison, 'I'm just sitting here...'

'So what exactly would it take?' said Ali, stunned by the admiral's comments. 'What in their few remaining hours could they possibly do to gain our protection?'

'I'm afraid that as far as these two go, it's going to be extremely hard to do anything to impress me for the foreseeable future.' Jimmy and Edison glanced at each other.

'What do you mean?' said Ali.

The Admiral pressed a button on his desk and two rather large GPOL officers entered the room.

'Impersonating a GPOL officer is an offence and is punishable by the law,' said the Admiral, looking weary and almost apologetic. 'I am sorry, Alianna. Take them away, officers.'

Edison and Jimmy looked shocked.

'No,' shouted Ali, 'you can't!'

The two large GPOL officers grabbed the boys by their collars and pulled them toward the door.

'But we need to save our planet,' said Edison. 'We've done nothing worth going to prison for!'

'Human,' said the Admiral, pointing to Edison's chest. 'That t-shirt is enough to get you tossed into the cells on its own.'

Edison didn't feel he could argue that point as he was manhandled out of the room.

'I'm so sorry,' said Ali as she sat on a bench inside Edison and Jimmy's cell. 'I don't know what else to say.'

Ali had managed to call in a few favours with the two GPOL officers that had been escorting Jimmy and Edison down to the cells and had checked them in herself, although one of them insisted on seeing the pair into their cell, smirking and making sarcastic comments all the way. This at least meant that they'd avoided having any personal belongings confiscated and had not been forced to wear inmate uniform.

Edison had his head in his hands and was kneading his forehead; Jimmy was standing poking the translucent energy-door with his fingers, completely amazed by it.

'We haven't much time left,' said Edison, looking up at the GPOL officer. 'Our delaying tactic won't keep the Repugnatrons distracted for long and then they'll be on their way again.'

'But what can we do?' said Ali.

'The main thing is to get us out of here,' said Edison. 'We can't do anything when we're locked up.'

'I'll try, but it may take time – yes I know we have none,' she added, seeing the look on Edison's face, 'but I'll try.'

'Ok. In the mean time, we need to go over my notes and see if there's anything we can use but I've got to say, it's not looking good.'

Edison reached into his pocket and pulled out two objects.

155

'Here,' he said, handing over the mobile phone to Ali. 'I've taken some video footage on this. It's low quality – can you have it improved somehow?'

She took the phone from Edison.

'I'll see what I can do, this thing's really primitive you know.'

'I'm not after High-Definition 3D, I just want to be able to see as much detail as possible. Oh, and I picked this up at Crackpot's house.' Edison handed over the small phial of glowing red liquid that he'd found half buried in the hallway and had dropped in his pocket, forgotten about until now. 'I don't know what it is or even if it's important – could you get it checked out too?'

'Odd,' said Ali, tilting the slow moving liquid back and forth. 'Leave it with me, I know someone that can help with this.'

She rose to her feet and walked toward the door.

'I know things look bad but it'll be okay,' she said.

Edison nodded dolefully but in his heart he seriously doubted it.

> Ten minutes later, Research and Development department, deck 902

Ali poked her head through the small hatchway that served as the dividing line between the normal people and the secretive and suspicious lab technicians. According to these lab technicians, the hatchway also represented a line of, on average, around ninety IQ points but as Ali was keen to point out, if popularity was also measured in IQ points, the whole lot of them would be in negative numbers.

'Oi! Is anyone here?' she shouted into the darkness beyond. She could just make out racks and racks of spare parts stretching into the murky distance but no signs of life. Did they really have to work in this semi-darkness or was it just to help build a "mysterious" vibe that they were trying - but failing - to pull off?

'Hey! Hello?' she said, smacking her hand on the hatchway. She'd have pressed the visitor's buzzer if the lab technicians had provided one, but the last thing they wanted to do is attract visitors.

'I'm giving you one more chance and then I'm coming in and then you'll be sorry!'

'Ahhh, is there any chance that someone in GPOL HQ *didn't* hear that?' said a nasally voice.

'Who said *that*?' demanded Ali.

'Only, our Aural Disturbance Detector just measured your yelling at a little over 115 decibels; prolonged exposure to such levels can cause permanent hearing damage, which means you are in contradiction of a hard-drive full of Health and Safety laws.'

'Torny, is that you?'

'Who's asking?'

'Show yourself or *I* will cause *you* permanent damage!'

An explosion of deeply curly red hair appeared from the darkness behind the counter as Torny and his white lab coat slipped into view. Torny was short for Tornado, a nickname he'd acquired thanks to his gravity-defying hairdo. Torny would tell you that he was

157

far too busy with intensely technical work to worry about his hair style where as everyone knew the truth was that nothing had actually been invented to date that would keep it in check.

'Ahh, ehm, Ali; very nice to see you!' said Torny, who added to the normal red lustre of his cheeks by blushing furiously. It was like dot-to-dot, only with freckles.

'Don't go giving me tha- hey, what do you mean, "Aural Disturbance Detector"?' she said, interrupting herself mid sentence. 'Do you really measure how much people yell at you? Seriously?'

'Erm, well, people do have a tendency to let their, ah, *urgency* get the better of them as it were.'

'You're some piece of work, Torny.'

'Thanks.'

'It wasn't a compliment.'

'Thanks all the same.'

She stared at Torny for a moment in bewilderment. He smiled back at her with wide eyes.

'Stop that, Torny.'

'Sorry.'

'Now listen, I need a favour. Two actually.'

'Okay, fine!'

'But you don't know what I'm going to ask.'

'Doesn't matter.'

'It doesn't matter?'

'Nope!'

'Okay, how about this: you empty your GPOL credit card into my account, leaving yourself with nothing whilst wearing a holo-shirt that says "kick me, I'm stupid!"'

'Ahhh, I can't actually do *that* one.'

'Why not?'

'Ahhh,' said Torny, looking sheepish, 'because I've spent all my money on gBay finding Fuzzy Bears memorabilia and don't get paid for another two weeks.'

Ali's face went from looking like it had been slapped to contorting with the effort of stifling laughter.

'Well,' she said when she had herself under control once more, 'I think we've both learnt something there. So, here's the real deal: I need you to extract the video content on this device and enhance it as best you can.' She handed over Edison's phone.

'Check this out,' Torny said with amazement. 'This things so bad that it's cool! I could get a month's wage for this on gBay!'

Ali leant in through the hatchway and grabbed Torny's lab coat by the collar.

'You won't!' she growled at him.

'I won't,' he agreed, shaking his head rapidly.

'I thought you'd see it my way.'

'Next?' said Torny.

'Next I need you to find out what this is.'

She handed over the small phial that Edison had given to her back in the detention cell.

'Hummm, interesting,' said Torny, holding the liquid container up close to his eye and flicking it with his other hand. 'I'll get right on it.'

'Good. And thanks,' said Ali who was turning to leave.

'But it'll cost you,' said Torny, who sounded a little unsure about this desperate course of action. Ali stopped dead in her tracks and pinned Torny with an

159

expression that clearly said: "now think carefully about your next few words because they could be your last".

'What'll it cost me, exactly?'

Torny's face split with a stupid grin, his teeth, which looked like he'd selected them from a boxing gymnasium's lost and found bucket, seemed to be jostling each other out of the way in order to see daylight.

'A date!'

Ali almost choked.

'I can quite honestly say that I'd rather eat a cake made from Astro-slugs.'

'I'll take that as a yes then, eh?'

Ali walked off.

'Eh?'

> The bridge, Repugnatron Battle Cruiser, stationary just past Jupiter

Fragnut and Gragnash sat before the open hatch that Edison had unscrewed on his 'inspection.' The two Repugnatrons were so wrapped up in wires that they looked like something a deep-sea trawler had hauled up in its nets just before being frantically tossed back to the depths where they belonged.

'Do you know where this bit connects to?' asked Gragnash, brandishing one of the long wires that projected from Crackpot's silver device. Fragnut turned the paper instructions over and over in his hands, a look of extreme agitation on his face.

'Erm...ahh...well...to be honest, I think there must be some parts missing...'

'That's it!' declared Gragnash. 'I've had enough! I don't care what that miserable GPOL squirt said - we need help. Drag that maintenance freak out of his cell and get it up here now.'

'But we've been working him quite hard lately. We don't want to, well, make it dead, almighty overlord, sir.'

'Quite right too; and while we have its family locked up, it will continue to work hard, Fragnut. Surely you don't care for these Techy Nerds all of a sudden, Lieutenant?'

'Absolutely not, sir!' said Fragnut. 'There should be no leniency for those that practise in abominable evil. If I had my way, sir, all of them would be hunted down and eliminated from all four corners of the universe!'

'Does the universe have corners?' enquired Gragnash.

'No idea, almighty overlord sir, but rest assured that if there were, there wouldn't be a corner dark enough for the Technoids to hide away in!'

Fragnut hovered up to the main view screen and pulled a few levers. They felt good in his hands after all that nasty technological wire business. The Lieutenant had only washed his hands once before in his life, but he doesn't talk about it – not even to his therapist - but this was almost the second time.

On the screen, a startled looking Repugnatron guard was yanked out of a deep sleep.

'Eh, wha?' groaned the guard.

'Send the Technoid slave up to the bridge immediately!' said Fragnut.

'Oh! Yes! Right away, sir,' said the guard, jumping to attention and going to unlock the prison cell door. 'Hummm, that'll be odd...' he said with a frown.

'Odd?' said Fragnut. 'What do you mean, odd?'

'Well, it seems as the door's unlocked and...' at this point the guard demonstrated the perfect dictionary definition of the word "gulp", 'the prisoner's missing, sir.'

'What!' bellowed Gragnash.

'Erm, I said that the door's unlo-'

'Shut up fool, I was being rhetorical!' blasted Gragnash.

'Rewhaticle, sir?' asked the guard.

'Fragnut,' said Gragnash calmly.

'Sir?'

'Grate-O-Matic that guard and get him to check the others – not in that order.'

'Right away, almighty overlord sir,' simpered Fragnut who, in times like these, realised just how fickle Gragnash's interpretation of the phrase "job satisfaction" could be.

A few minutes later, the guard appeared back on screen from outside another prison cell.

'Whoopsy,' said the guard, 'the others seem to be missing too,' which, aside from "Yikes! Is that a huge grater I can hear?" were his very last words.

> Cell 6406, Gamma section, GPOL HQ

Jimmy walked up and down in the cell whilst Edison sat back and imagined he was doing something really cool, such as throwing a tennis ball against the wall like Steve

162

McQueen — after all, you never know when someone may be looking in at you. Someone like the officer that escorted them to the cell; he was still hanging around, poking his head up against the semi-transparent door and jeering at them.

Internally, however, Edison was just as frustrated as Jimmy looked. They'd been cooped up in this cell for just over four hours now and they both knew that if the Repugnatrons had continued on after the GPOL ship had been ejected off the side of the battle cruiser, then Earth would be around one hour from complete extinction.

'We're not going to make it, are we, Ed?' said Jimmy, looking devastated.

Edison looked up at his normally irrepressible friend and his heart gave a lurch — if even Jimmy had lost hope then what hope could there be?

'Just…just don't think it, Jimmy. I'll sort it, I always do. I haven't let you down yet, have I?' Jimmy managed a weak smile but it didn't stop him pacing.

Suddenly the door melted away and Ali strode in.

'I'm sorry it's taken time, but I've managed to get you out.'

'What, really?' said Jimmy.

'Yes; I just needed to point out that if humans are not part of the gBay treaty, then they cannot be held accountable for gBay related crimes. They took a bit of convincing but eventually had to agree.'

'How did you get on with the video?' asked Edison, rising to his feet.

'I haven't been back yet, I came to get you out first. Come on, we'll go now.'

As they walked out of the cell, the large GPOL officer that had been loitering was waiting for them.

'What're you doing, going so soon, eh?' he said, looming over them.

'We're being moved,' said Edison. 'They caught us digging an escape tunnel under the bed. Another few minutes and we'd have been hijacking a lunar-shuttle out of here.' The officer's face dropped.

'What? A tunnel? Never!' he said, pushing passed Edison and running into the cell. Jimmy followed Ali as she walked away, shaking her head.

'Edison, are you coming?' she shouted over her shoulder.

'Of course,' he said with a sly grin. 'But I've got *pressing* business to attend to first.' With that, he casually pressed the red button on the outside of his cell. Having crashed to the floor in a heap, the paralysed officer had a perfect view under the bed.

'Damn,' he said, realising that there was no tunnel.

'Damn!' he repeated, realising there was no way of getting up and wringing Edison's neck.

> Research and Development department, deck 902

Reaching the hatch to the Research and Development department, Ali banged on the counter with her fist.

'Oi, Torny!' she bellowed.

164

'Ah ha!' declared the lab technician, who'd poked his head up Jack-in-the-box style from the other side of the hatch. Ali jumped back in shock.

'Torny! Why are you hiding back there?'

'Waiting for you!'

'Waiting? Why? Did you get that video enhanced?'

'Pha! Video, yes. I'm not interested in that. It's that liquid that's the star of the show.'

'Why,' said Edison, 'what is it?'

Torny glanced at Edison for a moment with a look of intrigue; this was his first close-encounter with a human.

'Well?' said Ali.

Torny's eyes glinted and he held up a finger, smiling in an excited schoolboy type of way. Dipping below the counter for a second, he resurfaced with a transparent cube around the size of a box of tissues. He then poked his fuzzy head out of the hatchway and looked up and down the corridor to ensure they were alone before pulling out the phial of red liquid.

'This,' he said, pointing at the cube, 'is one thousand times reinforced transparent titanium, it would take the force of fifty vaporisers set to "obliterate" without even as much as a scratch.'

'Thanks for the engineering lesson,' said Ali, 'now get to the point.'

Torny didn't seem in the least bit put out. Placing his hand under the counter, he then pulled out another phial of clear liquid.

'I'm going to put a tiny drop of pure water into the load chamber first.'

Aligning the water phial with a small hole at the top of the cube, he let a drop of water fall into the loading chamber where it dripped inside the cube.

'Now for the good part,' he said, giving everyone a view of his haphazard dentistry. Picking up Edison's phial with the red liquid, he tipped a small drop into the load chamber and put the cube quickly down on the counter.

'Erm, you'd better stand back,' he said and ducked out of site.

Edison, Jimmy and Ali had barely taken a step backward before the red liquid fell from the load chamber and into the cube, making contact with the tiny drop of water.

BOOm!

The cube rocketed off the counter, hit the top of the hatch (cracking the frame in the process) and fell to the floor with a thud.

'Ouch!' said Torny; obviously the cube hadn't fallen directly to the floor but had slowed its descent by bouncing off his head first. 'There,' he said, holding up the hideously contorted cube, 'HDF, or "Hydro Desolation Fluid". It reacts with water to cause an explosive chain reaction. This little beauty,' he said, waggling the phial with the red liquid, 'is enough to blow out three hundred floors if you were to drop it into the swimming pool on the Recreation Deck.'

Ali and Jimmy were both dumbstruck but Edison was already trying to work out the significance, if any, of the HDF.

'Where did you get it from anyway?' said Torny. 'This stuff's seriously out of bounds.'

'It was found at Crackpot's place,' replied Ali.

'What, *the* Crackpot from the Gallepede cluster?'

'Yes,' she said, still in shock from the demonstration.

'*The* Crackpot who used to work as a gBay programmer before picking up the largest amount of hacking court orders in GPOL history?'

Ali and Edison stared at each other.

'You didn't say Crackpot was a gBay programmer!' said Edison.

'I didn't know...I mean, I'd forgotten!' She smacked herself on the forehead.

'Hang about,' said Jimmy. 'If Crackpot's a programmer for gBay, can't he-'

'Hack in and cancel the sale of Earth,' finished Edison. 'What do you think?' he added, turning to Ali.

'There's only one way to find out,' she replied.

'Erm, hey! Ali!' shouted Torny as the three sprinted off down the corridor. 'What time should I pick you up tonight? Hey!'

Pressure Tactics

> The bridge, Repugnatron battle cruiser

It was no good; Fragnut had been trying to cheer up Gragnash for the last half hour but he was having none of it. Gragnash was seething about losing his maintenance slave and nothing, not even having his belly boils scratched, was going to pull him out of it.

'By the Stinky U-bends of Sinkorima Alpha' said Gragnash, looking down at the tangle of wires that was the still un-fitted "Thermal Spike Regulator". 'Lieutenant?'

'Yes almighty overlord, sir?'

'Bring me my nine-iron.'

'Right away, sir!'

Fragnut hovered over to a cupboard on the wall and opened the door by way of a chain-pulley on its right. When the door swung back, a rack of gnarly clubs in differing thickness and length presented themselves. Fragnut's hands hovered over the rack until he spotted the required club.

'Here you go sir. Nine-iron; a particularly good choice, if I may say so, sir.'

'Lieutenant?'

'Sir?'

'Would you like me to warm it up on your head?'

'Not exactly, sir, no.'

'Then shut it.'

'Immediately, sir. Subject closed. My lips are sealed. Consider me well and truly silenced-'

THWACK!

'I will indeed,' said Gragnash, who'd taken a test swing at Fragnut's nut.

'G...g...good weight, s...sir?' stammered the Lieutenant.

'Frightfully good. Excellent balance,' enthused Gragnash, studying the club fondly as if it were a part of his family, which was entirely possible.

Gragnash bent forward and lined up the Thermal Spike Regulator with his club. He made a few test swings whilst wiggling his backside (not a pretty sight — wiggling or not) and then pulled the club as far back as it would go.

'INCOMING!' he bellowed and let the club fly. It hit the Regulator with a crunch, sending it tumbling into the depths of the exposed console and its wires and pipes.

'There, fitted!'

'What now, sir?' said Fragnut, massaging the back of his head.

'Start up the engines again, Lieutenant, we've got a planet to mash!'

A wicked smile sprang up on Fragnut's face.

'Most certainly, sir!'

As the battle cruiser's monumental engines sparked back into life with all the commotion of an exploding volcano, an imperceptible shimmer cast itself over the stars above the Repugnatron ship. Had the Repugnatrons been looking for it, they'd still never have seen it. As it was, they weren't looking for it and neither were their proximity scanners, scanners that had been designed by Technoids, scanners that had been designed to *not* detect hidden Technoid spacecraft.

As the battle cruiser resumed its journey to Earth, unbeknown to the Repugnatrons, they were not alone...

> Cell L325, Delta Section, GPOL HQ

'Listen, Crackpot,' said Ali, 'time's short. Shorter than you. I'm not here to waste any of it because every second I'm here with you, Perry's on his own out there so you'll answer all of my questions quickly. Preferably before I've even asked them. Understood?'

'My client,' said a slick voice by the door, 'doesn't have to answer any of your questions until he has been officially charged with a specific offence relating strictly to the infringement of the gBay Treaty.'

The voice belonged to one Varicus Vain, an infamous lawyer throughout the Milky Way sector who, it was rumoured, was so good that he even got Sid "The slasher" Henderson off his murder charge by convincing the jury that he was at home at the time, tying little pink bows into his moon-poodle's hair.

'Is that so?' said Ali, turning toward Varicus with a dark look. So dark that even Varicus, who was used to working with some of the most fearsome beings in existence, felt he had to rearrange his pinstriped suit and clear his throat.

'Yes, that is so.'

'Get out.'

'Absolutely not! I'm here to represent my client and there's nothing that you can do to get me to leave!'

'Really?' said Ali. 'I'm no lawyer but as you rightly pointed out, we have not charged Crackpot with any offence yet and that means that he is not entitled to legal representation. *Guard*!' A GPOL officer entered through the door. 'Take this man away!'

Varicus struggled as the officer grabbed him by the lapels and frogmarched him toward the door. Edison stared at the back of Varicus's head as he went – it had another face set into it and this one appeared to be asleep. Varicus was from a race of lawyers that were so much in demand that they had no time to stop working and so have another face genetically grafted onto the back of their head, which can take over when the first one needed sleep. This is great news for the desperate late-night client, but bad news for those unaccustomed to paying a lawyers overtime charges.

'You can't do this!' said Varicus, his sleeping head spinning out of sight on its axis to be replaced with the awake version.

'Can and have,' said Ali as the door reappeared instantly behind the lawyer, shutting him out. As soon as they were alone Edison, Jimmy and Ali stood and stared at Crackpot, who was perched on the bed swinging his legs back and forth.

'Suspect intimidation!' he said, staring back. No one replied - they were going for pressure tactics. 'Nicey nicey hat,' Crackpot added, looking up at Jimmy and pointing with a purple fingernail, 'want to trade?'

'The only thing you've got to trade, Crackpot,' said Ali, 'is information so start talking.'

'You never said you were a gBay programmer,' said Edison.

'Human bean never asked!'

'Or a hacker,' put in Jimmy.

'Hacker? Me? Nopey wrong! Slander!'

'Really?' said Ali. 'Only, I've heard that you're one of the top five hundred hackers in this sector.' Crackpot looked offended.

'Five hundred, pah! Crackpot top of list! Oops...'

Ali smiled. 'Really? The best?' she said. 'I bet you couldn't hack into gBay.'

'Hack gBay? You wanting me to hack gBay?' said a startled looking Crackpot. Ali glanced up at the security cameras.

'You said that, Crackpot, not me.'

'Can't hack gBay. Impossible to hack gBay.'

'I don't know why you feel you need to talk about this, Crackpot,' said Ali, 'but I'll go with it for now.

Surely if anyone could hack gBay then you'd be able to, after all – you coded some of it.'

'Yeppy, Crackpot coded gBay and not me even can hack it! Think of it, girly – how many hackers in galaxy? How long gBay been live? How many hacks? None!'

All three exchanged looks; as much as they hated to admit it Crackpot did have a point, the statistics spoke for themselves.

'Why girly want to hack gBay anyway?'

'I ask the questions around here, perpetrator!' snapped the officer. 'Tell me why you were trying to leave Earth so quickly. You must've been desperate if you were trying to remove the GPOL securDoc from your ship.'

'Said before: holiday.'

'Liar! I'll tell you what I think. I think that you made some highly illegal deal with the Technoids, knowing that once the deal was done that GPOL would be after you and that you'd have to leave the planet quick or face a long stretch inside. Also, as you knew that we'd stopped your ship from being able to take off, you had the Technoids supply you with an anti securDoc device as part of the deal. To add to all this, there's the matter of the Repugnatrons, who as we speak are on their way to crush your adopted planet to dust!'

'Crackpot is knowing nothing about Repugnatrons crushing Earth!' said Crackpot, looking genuinely shocked.

'It could be true,' said Edison, 'he was already on the run when the sale went through...'

'You sold Earth on gBay?' said Crackpot, almost laughing. 'Oopsy! No wonder you wanting to hack system!'

'Just give us answers, Crackpot!' yelled Ali.

'Want to see lawyer,' he said, folding his arms across his chest. 'No more answery questions!'

'Come on,' said Edison, 'we're wasting our time here.'

For a moment, Ali looked like she was going to pummel Crackpot with her fists but she thought better of it and stormed to the door; it opened to allow her through.

'Your planet not so bad,' said Crackpot as Edison made to leave. Edison looked back at Crackpot, who seemed genuinely sad all of a sudden.

'Yeh, pity it won't stay that way.'

'Some people always look hardy way to do things, sometimes it helpy if you simply...change your mind.'

'Come on, Ed,' said Jimmy, 'Ali's storming off.'

Edison gave Crackpot a thoughtful glance before walking out of the cell.

'What do you think he meant, *change your mind*?' said Jimmy as they walked into Ali's living quarters in order to study the enhanced video footage extracted from Edison's phone.

'It's obvious isn't it?' said Ali. 'He just doesn't want to answer our questions.'

Edison looked around the room. It was a bit too clinical for his liking with all its white walls and furniture. It seemed to lack what his mother always referred to as "a woman's touch", but there was no way he was going to tell Ali that just in case she gave him "a woman's punch".

'I don't know,' he said, 'I almost got the impression he was trying to tell us something.'

'What, Crackpot, help us? Now I know you're mad.'

'Maybe,' mused Edison.

'He's in this up to his stumpy little neck,' said Ali, 'I just wish I could work out how.'

They took a seat on a white settee in the centre of the room and Ali typed a few commands into a virtual keypad that appeared on the surface of what looked like a simple coffee table. Just above the table appeared several three-dimensional icons just like the system built into her GPOL suit. She poked the one that looked like an envelope - this was her email inbox.

'Torny has mailed me the video file, I just hope it helps.'

When the inbox appeared, there was only one unopened email; Ali opened it and ran the video clip. It projected itself in two dimensions above the table.

'Cool!' said Jimmy, 'it's like being at the cinema!'

Not only was the image a good sixty inches in diameter but Torny's filtering had enhanced the originally small and grainy picture to a very acceptable standard. Edison watched in silence, studying the playback of the Repugnatron control console and the view screen with the gBay sale of Earth upon it.

'Is there any way we can get this translated?' he said, pointing at the playback of the Repugnatron view screen, which was unreadable.

'I'm no expert,' said Ali, 'but I'll give it a go.'

She froze the playback on a good image and then extracted it from the video. She then had the computer run an optical character reader program over the still to recognise any words from the Repugnatron view screen and replace them with something they could all read.

'Not bad!' said Edison as the converted image appeared.

'Thanks,' said Ali, with a rare smile.

As Edison poured over the picture, a new floating icon appeared by the side of the frozen Repugnatron view screen. Ali prodded it and the floating head and shoulders of Torny appeared above the table, he was beaming amiably. Edison couldn't help but suspect Torny had digitally enhanced his own image for his teeth were not quite as offensive as in real life and even his hair had come down a few categories to "very untidy".

'Yes, Torny?' said Ali.

'You said to let you know if there was any change with the Repugnatron battle cruiser.'

'Yes. And?'

'And there has been. It's moving toward Earth again.'

'Damn. How long have we got till it gets there?'

'At their present speed, around four hours, tops.' Edison, Jimmy and Ali stared at each other. 'You know, I'm normally far too busy doing very technical work to do this sort of thing,' said Torny.

'Yeh, thanks,' she said, knowing where this was leading.

'But just for you I'll make an excep-'

'Like I said, thanks...' She terminated the video link abruptly.

'That's not good, is it?' said Jimmy. Edison had his head in his hands; this was all his fault. If he hadn't bought the Neutrino Concentrator in the first place, none of this would be happening. How could he possibly live with himself if he caused the destruction of the entire human race?

'Won't Earth see them coming?' said Jimmy hopefully. 'They could hit them with a few missiles or something.'

'No,' said Ali, 'once their disintegrator is open, they're vulnerable to attack so they'll have cloaked themselves to Earth technology. Your planet won't have a clue what's coming.'

Ali said this last sentence with a barely contained bitterness. It was as if this whole affair was a rerun of the last days of her own planet and, just like then, it seemed there was no hope of stopping it from happening.

'What do you think, Ed?' said Jimmy, looking in an almost pleading way at his friend. 'What'll we do? What's your plan? It's going to need to-'

'Look,' snapped Edison, his face was flushed and he wore an expression that Jimmy had never seen before, which scared him for it was one of complete abandonment of hope. 'I haven't got a plan, all right? It's too late! Earth is going to be obliterated and it will go down in universal history as being entirely my fault!'

Both Jimmy and Ali watched in shock as Edison went off on a non-stop tirade, ranting and raving in an almost demented way about the end of the world. Ali stared with her mouth open for a while before she could take it no longer. She smacked Edison in the forehead with an open palm. He staggered backward, his seemingly endless monologue coming to a sudden halt.

'Okay,' she said, 'freak-out time over, yes?' Edison looked back at her with wide-eyed silence. 'Yes?'

Then it seemed as though a light had been flicked on inside Edison's head. His eyes lost their desire to leap out of their sockets and his face turned back to its normal hue.

'Yes. All done,' he said, feeling utterly foolish.

'Good, because there's a planet to save.'

With desperation well and truly setting in, the three took to searching through the online gBay laws in an effort to find some legal loophole that would force the Repugnatrons to abandon their attack. Ali even considered talking to Varicus Vain, but that thought only flashed across her mind for a nanosecond second before it was completely abandoned.

'Can't you blast them with some sort of death ray?' said Jimmy.

'Oh, why didn't I think of that,' said Ali, fixing Jimmy with one of her trademark glares. 'I could just borrow the GPOL Megatron Vaporizer-O-Matic Three Thousand and melt their ship right out of existence!'

'Really?' said Jimmy with a stunned expression.

'No, numb-nut!'

'Oh.'

'We're on our own with this, Jimmy,' said Edison. 'There's only us three and all we've got is the Recon ship, which, I assume, has no weapon capability?'

'Correct,' said Ali, 'and even if it did, to attack the Repugnatrons would be an act of war, something that all parties that sign up to the gBay Treaty agree not to do.'

'Including the Repugnatrons.'

'Yes,' said Ali.

'That was a convenient way to avoid reprisals after they destroyed your planet.'

'Exactly,' replied Ali, whose expression darkened and her gaze wandered somewhere unseen and unsightly for a moment.

'Let's just keep looking,' said Edison but a shriek of frustration from Ali told him that it was a waste of time.

'It's a waste of time!' she said. 'We've been over and over it, there's nothing that we can use, nothing that gives us even a slim chance of legally stopping this!'

A silence fell between them, there was now only two and three quarter hours before the lights went out on planet Earth for all time. No one looked at each other, they all retreated into their own grim, private thoughts and none of these thoughts were worth sharing.

Eventually the silence was broken. Someone had to do it and it may as well have been Jimmy.

'If only the Repugnatrons would...I dunno...just change their minds and go away.'

Ali snorted rudely. 'Change their minds? Don't you start; you sound just like Crack-'

She stopped mid sentence, it looked like someone had cut all the muscles that kept her face in place.

'Are you okay?' said Edison.

'hunnngkkg,' came the nonsensical reply.

'What?'

'Inordinate Sales Clause...' she muttered, still not regaining her normal facial control.

'Incontinent Santa Claus? Nope, you'll have to do better than that,' insisted Edison. Her eyes snapped back into focus.

'Inordinate Sales Clause... Inordinate Sales Clause!'

'Go on,' said Edison, 'say it again, I'm sure it'll make perfect sense this time...'

'I'd forgotten! I can't believe it! Listen,' said Ali, her voice quivering slightly.

'All ears,' said Edison, dryly.

'GPOL have spent so much time trying to sort out arguments over sellers taking huge sums of money for expensive but shoddy goods that gBay recently allowed purchasers of items with a perceived high value a cooling-off period after the sale.'

'In English?' said Jimmy.

'What she's trying to say,' said Edison, 'is that if planets in general are listed as expensive items, then the Repugnatrons may be able to retract their bid and pull out.'

'Exactly!' said Ali. 'But only-'

'-If we catch it in time, presumably?' finished Edison.

180

'Yes. You've only got a limited period – check the screen!'

'What am I looking for?' said Edison, moving closer to the projected image captured with his mobile phone.

'No idea, I've never seen the option before!'

Everyone scanned the image over and over but nothing looked likely. Then Edison pointed to a small, fuzzy blob at the bottom right of the screen.

'What's that? Can you zoom in on it?'

'Should be able to,' said Ali, who used her finger to position a square frame over the fuzzy section and then selected an enlarge option. The blob came into focus; it was a button with "ISC: Retract Bid" written across it and below was what looked like a frozen countdown timer reading nine hours, four minutes and twenty three seconds.

'Bingo!' said Edison.

'Not bad - for a human. I'll have to keep you around if you're going to be this useful.'

Edison held a smile for a moment before it suddenly dropped from his face like a lemming from a cliff top.

'What's wrong?' said Ali, seeing the change.

'I think I've just worked out exactly how Crackpot fits into this whole affair and I don't think you're going to like it...'

Crash Course

> The bridge, Repugnatron battle cruiser

Gragnash sat and surveyed the bridge from the comfort of his throne-like chair in the centre of the room. Not that it was a real chair, rather a grossly over designed parking space for his hover trolley as getting on and off it was far too much like hard work for a self respecting Repugnatron. As he sat and waited for his Lieutenant to reappear, Gragnash drummed his fingers on the arm of the chair.

'Ah, Fragnut!' he said, as the Lieutenant shot in through the door on his hover trolley.

'Alflighty overboard stir,' stammered Fragnut, who looked extremely green in the face from all his efforts to get back to the bridge in a timely manner.

182

'Have you been paddling your way here, Lieutenant? You look rather spent.'

'W...what, me, s...sir? No. Although, I especially I...liked your th...threat to bludgeon me t...to death if I was late. Very funny, that one, sir.'

'Hummm,' replied Gragnash as he quietly stowed his nine-iron back into his trolley. 'Now tell me, Fragnut, how goes the new prisoner?'

'Very well, sir. He seems to be in great discomfort; his screams are echoing all the way down corridors fifty nine through to sixty two.'

'Excellent. Don't let up on him, Lieutenant.'

'Wouldn't dream of it, sir.'

'Dream? Do you actually get any sleep, Fragnut?'

'No thanks to you, sir.'

'Quite so.'

Just then, an alarm sounded and a flashing message appeared in the centre of the view screen. Gragnash took on an expression of one who has just been woken from deep sleep by a large bucket of iced water in the face.

'By the Popping Pimples of Acneemia Virilus!' bellowed Gragnash, who was clutching at his chest. 'There'd better be a good reason for that - I think I've had an accident!'

Gragnash engaged his trolley's cleaning mechanisms whilst Fragnut approached the view screen.

'Yes, sir, good news indeed; we're almost there!'

'How long Lieutenant?'

'Just seventy five minutes, almighty overlord, sir.'

Fragnut pulled a few levers and on the screen, a large image of Earth appeared. Gragnash smiled in a way that would get a policeman scrabbling for his stun gun.

> Ali's quarters, GPOL HQ, Milky Way Sector

'Seventy five minutes!' said Ali in shock, 'you can't be serious!'

'Deadly,' said Edison with practised indifference. 'You saw the time on that video clip, it was seven and three quarter hours ago. Therefore, seventy five minutes until our cancellation window – and my planet – disappear for good.'

'I can't believe this,' she said, collapsing into a chair.

'Believe it,' said Edison. 'At least we've got something to work with now.'

'But what about Crackpot; you said you'd worked it out.'

'I need more time to think about that one,' he said, avoiding her eyes. 'I'll come back to it. For now, I've got jobs for you all.'

'What do you mean, *jobs*?' said Ali, who was quite unused to taking orders.

'Jobs, tasks, assignments, call them what you want if it makes you feel better but just don't argue, we haven't the time.'

Ali shot Edison a mutinous look but didn't argue.

'Jimmy?' said Edison.

'Yep!' replied Jimmy, who had seen the hope rekindle in Edison's eyes.

'I need you to find your way back to Ali's Recon Craft and bring back the Memory Cap as fast as you can.'

'No problem! Well, as long as I don't get lost...'

'Ali?' said Edison.

Ali entered some commands into the table and from a hatch a silver ball floated into the air, the same as the one that had led them to Crackpot's cell.

'Follow it and you won't get lost.'

'Now, Ali,' continued Edison, 'I need you to get hold of some disguises that we can use aboard the Repugnatron ship and they need to be good.'

She pulled a face. It looked like she'd just swallowed a raw egg.

'Problem?' said Edison.

'No,' said Ali, 'I know just the man for the job. Unfortunately. What about you?'

'If you can point me in the direction of a telephone, I need to make a call.'

'Fine – but no intergalactic calls, they'll cost me a fortune.'

'Don't worry this one's probably on your speed dial.'

Nineteen minutes later and Edison was pacing up and down like a caged lion. He had set his digital watch to count down and the display was now showing fifty six minutes left before he and Jimmy became the only living humans in existence. Just as he was about to

185

resort to sticking his head out of the door and staring up and down the corridor, Ali and Jimmy barged in.

'I found this one wandering around three blocks away. Apparently he got distracted by an AnyVend machine on the corner of corridor E334 and his Guide bobbed off without him.'

'Okay, okay,' said Edison, who was just pleased that they'd both turned up again. 'What've you got?'

They took a seat; Ali pulled a small bag from over her shoulder and placed it on the table.

'Is that it?' said Edison, seeing the size.

'What do you mean, "Is that it"? Don't even ask me what it's cost me to get this!'

'What's it cost you?' asked Jimmy, predictably.

'I said don't ask. Let's just say, my evenings are going to be taken up for the next few days. In fact, I'm really going to need to keep hold of one of these disguises if I want to retain some credibility.'

Ali unfastened the bag and pulled out a black all-in-one suit that looked like it belonged to a deep-sea diver. Edison was going to remark on how that must've been a tight fit when Ali pulled out three more. Both Edison and Jimmy were astounded.

'It's a BubbleBag; it uses Expanded Dimensional Technology to – never mind. It's big inside. These are Chameleon suits, I got one each, just in case.'

'Four?' noted Edison.

'Yes, four,' said Ali warningly, almost reading his mind. 'Like I said - one each.'

'Fine,' said Edison curtly, not wanting to waste even a second of time. 'I assume they actually do something and are not just, well, black?'

186

Ali unclipped her GPOL utility belt and stepped into one of the suits. It was baggy to start with but tightened to fit perfectly. On the wrist was a system similar to the one on the regulation GPOL suit, a small three dimensional computer display system.

'Torny,' she started and then grimaced as she saw the expressions on Edison and Jimmy's faces – they'd guessed why she was going to be busy for the next few evenings, 'Torny went off on one about how these things work in detail, but basically it's this: instead of reflecting light normally like all other objects, which allows us to see them as they really are, the suit rejects light and emits its own.'

'What's that mean?' said Jimmy. Edison smiled; he'd already worked it out.

'It means,' continued Ali, 'that you can get the suit to project any image you want from the installed database, making you look like a completely different being or object even. It also comes with a scanner for updating the database.'

'Let's see it work,' said Edison.

Ali accessed the wrist computer and scrolled down a list of options until she found the one she wanted.

'Here we go.' In an instant she had vanished and was replaced with a grotesquely accurate representation of a Repugnatron, complete with hover trolley, although it was sitting on the floor.

'Perfect!' said Edison.

'What about the whole hovering thing?' asked Jimmy.

'Not a problem,' said Ali, who'd just returned back to her normal self. 'We can use the anti-gravity device which comes as standard on all GPOL suits.'

Jimmy nodded as he remembered how Perry and Ali had floated up to Edison's window after landing their spaceship in his garden.

'What about our voices?' asked Edison.

'Don't worry, this suit is fully loaded. It has a combined translator and voice box manipulator built into the neck; whatever life form you choose from the list, your voice will be changed to sound like one of them including speaking their language.'

'And you, Jimmy, did you manage to get the Memory Cap?' asked Edison.

'Certainly did!' said Jimmy, and he pulled out the device from where he'd hidden it up his jumper.

'Great. Now, I'm going to need some sort of portable terminal, like a laptop or whatever you have.'

Ali reached into the pouch on her GPOL utility belt and handed over what looked to Edison like a pen.

'This looks like a pen,' said Edison with a quizzical look. Ali rolled her eyes.

'Typical human.'

Putting the device on the table, she pushed a button on the end. Edison expected to see a nib extend from the other side but instead a virtual screen projected itself from the top length whilst a virtual keyboard projected itself along the front edge.

'Impressive,' said Edison. 'It even feels like real keys,' he said, poking the keyboard.

'That's because it beams tactile responses directly into your brain to make you think the keys are actually there. Now, are you going to tell us what's going on here?'

'Yeh, Ed, what's the plan?' said Jimmy.

'Okay. I've tried to keep it simple to increase the chances of it working.'

'Reassuring...' said Ali.

'Quiet. Now, firstly we get back to the Repugnatron ship – *quiet*!' he said, seeing Ali's desperate attempts to point out problems with his plan. 'When we're there, I'm going to make my way to the bridge whilst you and Jimmy create a distraction.'

'How?' Ali managed to squeeze in.

'Simple, you're going to have a bar brawl.'

'Excellent!' said Jimmy.

'Ridiculous!' said Ali.

'Apparently it's built into the Repugnatron genetic makeup that they can't resist a fight so the bridge should be abandoned and this should allow me to hack into their Neutrino Concentrator, crack their username and password and then cancel the purchase. Once you've started your fight, one of you needs to slip away and find Perry. Any questions?'

'You're insane!' said Ali.

'That's a statement, not a question.'

'Okay, firstly, how do you plan on getting back onto the Repugnatron ship? In case you've forgot, they tried to blast us off the last time we were there!'

Edison made to answer but a sound from the door alerted them to a waiting visitor. Ali walked over and opened it.

'Gordon?' she said incredulously. 'What are you doing here?'

The large UPS deliveryman smiled widely and looked over at Edison.

'You ready to go?'

'You *can't* be serious!' said Ali.

'Entirely. Almost ready, Gordon - we just need to make a stop off on the way out.'

Ali didn't know whether to laugh or cry.

'Have you even considered that even if we do get back, even if we do clear the bridge then you've still no idea how to hack into the Repugnatron's systems?'

'I *have* considered that.'

'And?'

'Hence our stop off. You need to show me how this thing works on the way there,' he added, lifting the Memory Cap from the table.

'On the way where?'

'Crackpot's cell - he's about to give me a hacking crash course.'

'Nopey no! Crackpot not help human bean. Nope.'

Crackpot sat in his cell with an attitude of complete defiance. It would've looked a lot more impressive if his feet had actually reached the floor and were not swinging back and forth.

'Are you sure?' asked Edison.

'Sure!' replied Crackpot.

'How about if...' Edison made a show of thinking deeply, 'we were to give you this?' He plucked Jimmy's hat from his head and held it out to Crackpot.

'Me takey hat first!' said Crackpot, whose eyes had lit up at the offer. Edison rubbed his chin.

'And then you'll help?'

'Maybe.'

'Oh, I'm sure you will,' decided Edison and handed the hat to Crackpot, who plonked it straight on his head.

'Ha! Nicey hat, all mine!'

'It's a little crooked, Crackpot,' said Edison. 'Here, let me.'

Reaching over, Edison pushed a button through the material that triggered the Memory Cap, which was hidden inside. Crackpot's feet stopped swinging immediately and his face became blank.

'Are you sure you set that thing to record and not playback?' whispered Ali, looking around nervously.

'Of course,' confirmed Edison.

'Quick, say the trigger words before we all get locked up.'

Edison lent close to Crackpot's face.

'Hacking. Repugnatron. Spaceship systems. HDF.'

'HDF?' said Jimmy with a frown.

'I'll explain later,' replied Edison.

Crackpot's lips began to wobble and he made a rapid burbling noise as the Memory Cap went to work. It was only Jimmy standing at Crackpot's side that stopped him from pitching head first off the bed.

After a few moments, it was all over. The Memory Cap stopped probing the dark crevices of Crackpot's mind and control of his lips began to return to him. Edison quickly removed the hat from Crackpot's head.

'Heh? What? Is someone saying something to Crackpot?' said the prisoner as he regained consciousness and started to rub his head.

'No,' said Edison with a sigh, 'we're all done here.'

'But Crackpot feely different.'

'What's he mean?' said Ali in Edison's ear.

'I'm sure it's nothing,' said Edison. 'He's just a little confused, that's all.'

'Well let's go then, quick.'

'If you two could just wait outside,' he said, motioning toward Jimmy and Ali, 'I've just got a bone to pick with Mr Crackpot here.'

Ali, having no idea what he meant, gave him a deep frown but followed Jimmy out of the cell without further comment. After all, time was not so much ticking down as in freefall.

Ten precious minutes later, Edison reappeared through the cell door. Jimmy, Ali and Gordon were all waiting.

'You took your time!' snapped Ali.

'Didn't your mother ever tell you that patience was a virtue?' replied Edison.

'Didn't *your* mother ever tell you never to look down the wrong end of a fully charged Vaporiser?'

Edison didn't reply. He felt the only cool retort was to raise his right eyebrow for a moment and just leave it at that. It's what Mr Spock would've done.

Edison, Jimmy and Ali waited up front in the cockpit of the UPS delivery ship whilst Gordon and Flash argued outside in the hanger with GPOL officials about overdue parking fees and illegal thruster-clamp removal. Edison was drumming his fingers on one of the hundreds of brown boxes that were piled up in a seemingly random order all around the cockpit.

'Can't you stop that,' said Ali, 'it's making me nervous.'

'Is it? Well maybe I'm a little over sensitive but letting the Repugnatrons get even closer to blending my home planet into some sort of bizarre space-shake makes *me* a little nervous.'

Ali tutted; he was right but to come back with nothing was against her better nature. 'So what about Crackpot,' she said. 'You told us you knew how he fitted into all this?'

Edison didn't answer for a moment; Ali saw the mental falter and became suddenly suspicious.

'What? What's going on?'

Edison sighed.

'It's only a guess but I think it's a pretty accurate one. It began when Torny told us what was in that phial we found at Crackpot's house. I started thinking that maybe the phial was only a sample. I then put that together with the involvement of the Technoids and how they seemed to be helping Crackpot leave Earth in a hurry by giving him the device to bypass your SecurDock system. Maybe they were paying him in return for a large quantity of the Hydro Desolation Fluid.'

'But why? What would they want with it?' said Ali.

'That's what I wondered until you mentioned how all the members of the gBay Treaty had agreed never to wage war on any other Treaty members. This would mean that the Technoids couldn't attack the Repugnatrons in order to settle a score without serious repercussions.'

'What score?'

'When I was aboard the Repugnatron ship I saw a prison cell with five creatures in it. Creatures that I didn't recognise at the time. But when you joked about keeping me around if I was going to be useful, it suddenly occurred to me that this was exactly what Gragnash has been doing – he's been keeping Technoids captive in order to ensure his ship runs smoothly and the Technoids don't like it a bit. So, they plan to beam aboard a few dozen barrels of HDF when nobody's looking.'

'Just wait a minute,' said Ali with a confused expression, 'what you're saying is that the Technoids are planning to destroy the Repugnatron's ship in payback for kidnapping and mistreating some of their people?'

'I think so, yes.'

'Don't be stupid - they can't. Not only would it be traced back to them but they'd also be killing their own people in the cells!'

'And didn't you say that nothing can beam on or off the Repugnatron ship?' said Jimmy.

'Okay, hear me out,' said Edison. 'Another thing I noticed when I was on the Repugnatron ship was that they were having escape pod malfunctions, resulting in some of the pods detaching and floating off.'

'So?' said Ali.

'So I don't think this was a coincidence. I think that the Technoids were deliberately letting them loose whilst pretending to fix other problems.'

'Why?' said Ali, her voice getting more and more agitated.

'For two reasons. Number one: to escape without being noticed. When I left the Repugnatron ship, I passed the same cell – the prisoners were missing. There'd been a "pod malfunction" a few minutes earlier but nothing was done to scan the pod when it floated away as it'd been happening a lot. I think that the Technoids were in it and if you check your Recon craft's radar data, I'd be willing to bet that the pod had vanished shortly afterward as a hidden Technoid craft picked them up.'

Ali was starting to look very concerned at this point; Edison's theory did seem to be holding some water.

'And the second reason?'

'Jimmy was right – you can't beam onto the Repugnatron ship for security reasons but, as I mentioned before, you *can* beam into the escape pods from anywhere – from onboard the ship or from outside. This is so that even if the pod leaves without you, you still stand a chance of getting aboard.'

'And?' said Ali, whose voice was now shifting to one of quiet resignation.

'And,' continued Edison, 'I think the second reason the Technoids were letting the escape pods loose was so that when the Repugnatrons got within mashing distance of a life-rich planet, they would beam the HDF into one of the pods and remotely detach it,

195

knowing it would be completely ignored whilst it flew directly to the nearest planet capable of sustaining life, just as they are programmed to do. The Technoids knew that as soon as the escape pod ditched into an ocean, the barrels of HDF would start a massive chain reaction that would destroy the planet, taking their enemies, the Repugnatrons, with it.'

Ali looked like she'd been slapped. Jimmy made an odd whistling noise.

'It would look like an accident,' he said. 'There'd be no tracing it back to the Technoids.'

'No,' agreed Edison.

'So even if we manage to stop the Repugnatrons from crushing Earth,' said Jimmy, 'it'll still get destroyed by the HDF!' Edison's silence was taken by all as an agreement.

'Why didn't you tell me this earlier!' demanded Ali.

'Because you'd have throttled Crackpot in his cell and we'd all have been locked up.'

'Throttled him? I'd have lashed him to a weather drone and fired him at the nearest gas planet!'

'That's my point, right there.'

Ali didn't say anything else for a while; she seemed to be staring straight through the floor of the UPS ship, her dark eyes were glistening with tears.

'You okay?' said Edison.

She looked up at him with a face that he would never thought her capable of owning.

'You've got to stop this, Edison,' she said, tears streaming down her face.

'Well, I've been think-'

'No! You've really *got* to stop it! If that ship blows, then I'll lose my-'

'- Partner, I know.'

Ali took a deep breath. 'Brother. I'd be losing my brother.'

Edison and Jimmy stared at her.

'Perry's your brother?' said Edison with astonishment.

'Yes,' she said weakly.

'Cripes,' said Jimmy. 'Next you'll be telling us that the Admiral's your father!'

Ali didn't say anything but her look said it all.

'Well,' said Edison, 'hack a system I've never used, save an entire planet from a fiery extinction and rescue the Admiral's son from an explosive death. We're going to have quite an afternoon.'

At this point Gordon thrust his head around a pile of boxes and stuck his thumb up.

'Ten minutes and we're off, okay?'

'Okay,' said Edison. 'What's the hold up?'

'Oh, Flash has got some GPOL squirt – no offence, Ali - in a headlock but he thinks the situation should resolve itself pretty soon judging by the colour of the bloke's face.' Gordon disappeared again.

Edison took the Memory Cap and the GPOL computer "pen" from within the Bubble Bag.

'That gives me ten minutes to learn everything about hacking that our wayward Salamanderine friend has to offer and write a program to crack the Repugnatron's gBay password.'

'And the Technoids?' said Ali.

197

'Well,' said Edison hesitantly, 'there are two choices. One is to rewrite the piece of system code that disengages the escape pods and stop them from releasing. The HDF would be safe as long as it doesn't come into contact with water. The other is to find someone willing to hold down the escape pod's built-in self-destruct button with their finger until the thing blows itself up.'

'It has to be a finger?' said Jimmy.

'Yes,' replied Edison, 'it's a safety feature, if you can believe it. Stops you resting your coffee cup on it and vaporising yourself by accident.'

'Not much of a choice then, is it?' said Ali cynically.

'Nope,' said Edison, 'it's going to have to be the first option...'

'There sounds like there's a "but" coming.'

'But,' confirmed Edison, 'I won't be able to do that until I'm directly connected to the Repugnatron system.'

'Oh great!' said Ali. 'Well I hope you're a fast learner because I'm not going to brawl with every Repugnatron on the entire ship whilst you're sitting there on page one of the "Spaceship Operating Systems for Dumbo's" manual.'

Edison turned and looked at the GPOL officer with a slight smirk.

'You know, your sarcasm's really coming on. I attribute it to my influence. I think that if you were...I don't know...say, more fun than a tooth extraction, we'd be friends.'

'Shut it and get that thing on.'

Edison positioned the Memory Cap over his head having already set it to "Playback".

'Ready?' said Ali. Everyone knew that the entire plan was useless if this crucial part didn't work and no human had ever attempted to blast information into their brain in this way before.

'Good luck, Ed,' said Jimmy.

Edison reached up and pressed the trigger button. Everyone held their breath – including Edison, but for him this was not a conscious decision, it was just that his brain was too busy being bombarded with information for it to remember to breathe at the same time.

For nearly fifty seconds, Edison shook as the Memory Cap went to work, filling his sponge-like brain with years' worth of Crackpot's programming experience. Then, just when Jimmy and Ali were exchanging worried looks, the shaking stopped and Edison pitched forward off of his box and landed in a heap on the floor. For a few moments he remained utterly still, then...

'Nice of you to catch me,' he said with an effort.

'Woops,' said Ali sarcastically.

Edison climbed back onto his box, rubbing his bruised forehead.

'Blimy, are you okay, Ed?' asked Jimmy.

'Forget that,' said Ali, 'did it work? Have you learnt anything?'

Edison turned on the portable terminal, its holographic keyboard and screen casting a bluish hue over the surrounding boxes.

'Well?' said Ali.

Edison's hands hung over the virtual keys as if waiting for a starting pistol. But nothing happened. No blinding flash of inspiration. No overwhelming urge to type. Nothing.

'I knew this wouldn't work!' said Ali. 'It could take weeks for the information to filter into his conscious brain – if at all!'

As she ranted on about the stupidity of the plan and how everything was doomed to failure, Jimmy watched Edison as he gingerly poked one key, and then another, and then another in a snail-slow rhythm.

'Shush!' he said as Ali seemed to be reaching a head-aching crescendo. 'He's doing it!'

Ali fell quiet as she too watched Edison's hands poke slowly at the keys, one after the other. As they stared, Edison became quicker and quicker until they were zipping across the keyboard as quickly as they did back in his own bedroom.

'So?' said Ali anxiously. Edison looked up and raised both eyebrows at her.

'You know, this keyboard is truly terrible...'

Twelve and a half minutes later Flash and Gordon reappeared in the cockpit looking very pleased with themselves.

'Can we go now?' snapped Ali.

'Problems sorted?' asked Edison without looking up from the holo-screen or breaking his typing stride.

'Oh, yeh!' said Gordon. 'He wanted to impound our ship but then Flash here,' and he slapped his partner on his large, round shoulder, 'Flash threatened to read out over the loud speaker the guy's personal gBay order list for the last twelve months. This seemed to fix the problem super quick for some reason. So, you lot ready to leave?'

Edison stopped typing and looked at Jimmy and Ali. 'This is it, no turning back. There's a lot on the line with this one, Jimmy. More than ever before.' Jimmy nodded dolefully as he thought about their last big job; their pursuit of money seemed absurd in light of their next objective – to save the world. 'Everyone ready? Got everything?'

Jimmy and Ali nodded.

'Buckle up back there!' Gordon shouted over the whine of the starting engines; he and Flash were strapping themselves into the only two chairs on the ship. Jimmy frowned and looked down at what he was sitting on – a cardboard box.

Gordon and Flash pushed their dark glasses further up their noses simultaneously. Flash grasped the flight controller tightly in his right hand.

'I feel the need...' he said, looking over at Gordon.

'The need...' added Gordon.

'For speed!' they finished in union.

At the back of the cockpit, Edison was adding the finishing touches to his rousing speech.

'Well, let's go and save humanity,' said Edison. 'Oh, and guys – let's make it look professional!'

Up front, the flight clearance light illuminated and, with a grating, grinding crunch, Flash jammed the flight controller as far forward as it would go without breaking off. At the back, Edison, Jimmy and Ali were tossed into a seriously unprofessional heap beneath a pile of brown boxes.

Countdown to Disaster

> The Bridge, Repugnatron Battle Cruiser, planet Earth's back yard...

As the Repugnatron ship slipped undetected past the Moon, Gragnash ordered the Disintegrator's filter traps be emptied to ensure maximum capacity. At the pull of a chain, three million metric tonnes of indigestible space debris jettisoned out of the rear of the battle cruiser and peppered humanities last outpost in a monumental hailstorm, obliterating Man's first extraterrestrial footprints in its wake, footprints that should have endured for millennia.

'Let me see it, Fragnut,' said Gragnash, his four eyes glinting and his mouth salivating. 'On screen!'

Fragnut manipulated the levers before him and the view screen crackled to life, showing in magnificent clarity the crescent shaped beauty of planet Earth as it moved gently through its orbit of the Sun.

'Fragnut, someone's been there already – half's missing!'

'Err, actually almighty overlord sir, it's just in the shadow of this moon. We're coming in at an angle as it were, to avoid blocking out the sunlight. No need to give them an early warning - this lot've got some nasty little explodey things connected to some rather itchy trigger fingers, sir.'

'Of course, yes – I knew that...'

'I'm slowing the approach so we don't smash into it. On your supreme command, I will increase the Mashing Teeth to maximum capacity, sir.'

'I command it, Lieutenant!'

Fragnut performed an excited little bow and turned to the console whereby he pulled a large and well-worn lever. On the outside, the monolithic rings of teeth within the Disintegrator began to blur with deadly speed.

Back on the bridge, an alarm bell prematurely ended Fragnut's odd little 'war' dance.

'It seems we have an incoming craft, sir.'

'Destroy it and then send out a warning – in that order,' said Gragnash, showing little interest.

'But almighty overlord sir, it's UPS – it could be a delivery for me...'

Gragnash let out an agitated noise.

'Oh, let them in but make it quick or I'll beam you onto this planet right before I mash it to a pulp!'

As Flash brought the UPS delivery ship out of Hyper-speed, his instrument panel lit up like a community playing field on bonfire night.

'Hold on back there, we've got an uncharted debris field dead ahead!'

Before Edison had time to even say 'Hold onto what, exactly?' Flash had thrown the unwilling ship into a series of rolls, banks and dives, tossing anything and anyone not buckled down around the cabin like a rag doll in a spin dryer. The ship's engines were making awful groaning noises as they fought to keep up with the demands that the crazy pilot was making of them and at one point cut out completely, leaving them on a high speed collision course with a hunk of super-dense iron ore the size of a hockey pitch before firing back up at the last second and pulling them out of the way.

'Everyone okay in the back?' said Gordon, turning around in his chair with a huge grin.

'I'll answer when my broken ribs have healed and my lungs have re-inflated,' groaned Ali.

'Yeh; where did you learn how to fly,' said Jimmy, 'the Playstation academy?'

'Listen,' said Flash, 'there ain't no academy that'll teach you how to fly like me and Gordon!'

'I can believe it,' mumbled a pile of boxes that turned out to be Edison. After climbing to his feet and checking that he was all there, he staggered over to the flight controls. 'Can you see them?'

'Can we ever!' said Gordon, who pointed to a view screen. On it was the truly shocking sight of the Repugnatron ship and its mind-bogglingly huge Disintegrator. To the battle cruiser's left was Earth; sitting there like a circus entertainer preparing to place its head deep into a lion's crushing jaws. Edison's face paled. He checked his watch.

'We've got time to cancel the sale yet. Thirty minutes. Have they cleared you to dock?'

'Yes,' said Flash, 'a few seconds ago.'

'Good. Take us in.'

Flash nodded and plunged the control stick to its furthest-most extent, sending Edison flying back into his pile of boxes at the rear of the cockpit.

It took less than a couple of minutes to catch up with the Repugnatrons and this time it was done without any acrobatics, to Edison's relief. As the UPS delivery ship came in to dock, a horrendous screeching of metal on metal told Flash that he'd skidded to a perfect stop just over the docking hatch.

'Touchdown!' said Gordon, giving his partner a high-six.

'Right,' said Edison, 'everyone get ready – we're going in!'

Flash yanked open the UPS delivery van's sliding door to reveal the dark, dank Repugnatron corridor. As soon as it was confirmed that the sewer-like tunnel was deserted, Edison, Jimmy and Ali descended from the delivery ship and spread out along the access way.

'Anti-gravity systems on,' said Edison. They all activated the GPOL personal anti-gravity devices on

206

their belt, making them rise from the floor. 'Arm your disguises,' he added as he floated in to the air.

With a crackle of static, all three turned instantly into Repugnatrons causing even Flash to stare in shock.

'There's no time to waste,' said Edison, pointing his four eyes in the direction of Jimmy and Ali. 'Go!'

Ali looked at Edison with an expression that was totally unrecognisable to him.

'Good luck,' she said simply.

'And you. Both of you. Be careful.'

With that, they all moved off down the corridor, Jimmy and Ali taking the first junction on the right whilst Edison and Flash, carrying a box under one arm, carried straight on.

Ten minutes later Edison and Flash had reached the round sliding doorway to the bridge.

'You go in and do your thing as normal,' said Edison, 'I don't want them getting suspicious. When you come out, I'll go in.'

'Right you are, my floating repugnant friend!' said Flash and he approached the bridge. Both Fragnut and Gragnash turned as the door swung back and revealed the approaching UPS man.

'Urgh,' said Gragnash, leaning over to whisper in Fragnut's ear, 'there are some truly ugly alien races out there...'

'I agree, sir,' replied Fragnut with a sneer.

'I've a delivery for a Lieutenant Fragnut,' said Flash, tossing the box onto a nearby console.

'That's me!' said Fragnut with glee.

'Right,' replied Flash, looking the Lieutenant up and down with contempt. 'Well, spit on the pad,' he added, pulling his authentication device from out of his jacket pocket and pointing it toward Fragnut.

'My pleasure...' smirked the Lieutenant.

Three seconds later and the deliveryman's entire right arm was coated in a gooey, green gunk.

'Yuk!' he said, flicking a bucketful of the residue onto the floor.

'Now see yourself out before I set the dogs on you!' barked Gragnash.

'Have we got any dogs, almighty overlord sir?' asked Fragnut.

'No. Mental note, Lieutenant: when all this is over, get some dogs.'

'Certainly, sir!'

When Flash reappeared in the corridor, Edison was holding his wristwatch to his face.

'All yours,' said Flash, keeping his arm as far away from his nose as possible.

'Err, thanks,' said Edison, staring at Flash's sleeve.

'Don't ask — I must remember to get this little episode wiped from my memory.'

'Come and see me when this is all done and I might just be able to help you with that,' replied Edison.

'You know,' said Flash with a grave expression, 'you're welcome to come back with me and get off of this festering pile of slime infested junk.'

Edison glanced up at him with a determined look and shook his head.

'I'd love to, Flash, but I've only got fourteen minutes to save the Earth.'

Flash stared at him for a moment before his face broke out into a wide grin.

'Ha! I love your style, Earth boy.' He held out a large hand — thankfully, thought Edison, it was the one that was dry. He shook it. 'Good luck, Edison Fox, and don't forget — even if you fail, I still want payment!'

'Thanks, Flash, I'd be the same; but remember the last part of the deal...'

'No problem, little fella'!'

As the big man squelched off up the corridor in the direction of his ship, Edison readied himself for his part. He could only hope that Jimmy and Ali had done *their* part.

On the bridge Gragnash was in fits of hysterical laughter. He was holding up Fragnut's pink heart-shaped "I love Uranus" pillow just out of reach of the deeply embarrassed Lieutenant, who was attempting to swipe it back without tipping off his hover trolley.

'Yes, very amusing, sir,' said Fragnut tersely, 'but may I?'

'No,' replied Gragnash, who then popped the pillow underneath his sweaty backside. 'Ah, such comfort, Lieutenant!'

Fragnut's arms fell limply to his side — not even tossing the thing into the SupaWash 2000 for a week on Filth Annihilation Setting eighty three was going to make him want that back.

Just then, the door to the bridge swung open and a fully disguised Edison charged in at speed. Gragnash gave him a piercing look.

'Urm, Gragnash, sir,' began Edison, 'I've been told to-'

'WAIT!' bellowed Gragnash.   Edison's heart lurched. 'What's your name?'

'Erm...Picard...'

'Eh? Kickhard? Good name. Now, Kickhard, you haven't given the Repugnatron salute! Do you want to be sent to the Grater?'

Edison froze, his mind digging deep in the repository of scam-saving retorts but nothing seemed to cover this eventuality.   Desperate times call for desperate measures; he'd have to go back to the playground for inspiration.   In a single flowing movement, Edison merged together all of the rude hand gestures that he could think of during his informative years in education and let Gragnash have them. Gragnash raised his hairless eyebrows.

'Rarely have I seen it done so accurately. Well done. Now, what's your business?'

'Sir! There's a brawl down in the bar, sir!'

'Really?' said the Repugnatron with excitement.

'Yes, sir – a really bloody one too!'

Gragnash looked tempted.

'Almighty overlord sir, I think it best if we carry on with our important business first,' said Fragnut.

'Maybe you're right...' said Gragnash.

'But sirs,' said Edison, 'there's body parts everywhere! It's a real gore-fest!'

'At least let's check it out from here on the view screen to make sure it really is that good, sir,' said Fragnut.

'Oh I suppose so,' moaned Gragnash.

Edison's stomach started to squirm – he was afraid of this. It was the reason that he'd sent Jimmy and Ali down to the bar in the first place instead of just lying about the fight. He crossed his Repugnatron fingers.

'On screen, Lieutenant!'

> Outside the "Slam and Brag" Repugnatron Bar

'So how're we going to do this?' said Jimmy as he and Ali stared at the door to the bar.

'It shouldn't be that hard, just insult someone's girlfriend – that usually does it.'

'Okay. Insult girlfriend. No problem.'

'Ready?'

'Ready!'

Ali pushed open the door to the bar and hovered in, closely followed by Jimmy. The room was huge with a seemingly endless counter extending away from them on the right and hundreds upon hundreds of tables scattered around the floor, most of which had a Repugnatron slumped across it in a deep, drink induced sleep. Altogether, it was very quiet and subdued.

'This may be harder than we thought,' said Jimmy.

Ali nodded. 'You take the counter and I'll work the floor.'

Jimmy moved along the counter looking for a Repugnatron who was neither in a coma or had its mouth open under a constantly running beer tap. Eventually he found one that must have only just finished his shift and was not yet drunk. The

Repugnatron saw him coming and stuck his thumb in his right ear and wiggled his fingers in a common, lower-ranking Repugnatron greeting.

'May your belly boils be bursting with bile, comrade.'

Jimmy stared at the Repugnatron.

'Urm...boils...burst...you too...'

The Repugnatron nodded wearily whilst pouring out a tankard of lumpy, stagnating "Slam and Brag" house beer.

'Had a bad day?' asked Jimmy, warming himself up before the insulting.

'Real bad. Been guarding that disgusting human creature in C-wing. What a noise. Still, it'll give out soon, no doubt.'

Jimmy thought all his luck had come at once – which is not a necessarily a good thing when you're on a spaceship that without a lot of luck will be blown to smithereens anytime soon. There had been no real plan for finding out where Perry was being held - not that this mattered if Edison couldn't stop the escape pod full of HDF detaching itself and ditching into the sea.

Jimmy looked over at Ali; she was poking various sleeping Repugnatrons but was getting no response. She shrugged back at him. It looked like it was up to him. He put on his best aggressive look.

'I...ah...saw your girlfriend the other day. I've got to say, she's a real space moose!'

The Repugnatron looked over at him.

'Oh, ya' think so do ya'?'

'Yeh,' replied Jimmy. 'I've scraped better looking things off the bottom of my hover trolley than that!'

'Is that right?'

'Yes, as it happens,' said Jimmy, whose heart was beginning to race. 'She smells *so* bad I thought the septic tank pipes had ruptured.'

The Repugnatron's four eyes widened. Jimmy braced himself for impact.

'That...that's the nicest thing anyone's ever said about my girl. Thanks, comrade!'

Jimmy's jaw dropped – the Repugnatron's eyes were even brimming with tears.

'Erm, that's okay,' he mumbled.

'Call me Scaremonger, comrade.'

Jimmy looked over at Ali, she had resorted to slapping the sleeping Repugnatrons but even that was doing no good. Jimmy was getting desperate.

'You know, she really does *stink*! Pooee!'

'Enough,' said the Repugnatron, 'you're too kind.'

Jimmy threw his hands in the air in frustration, wobbled violently and grabbed for the counter to regain his balance. In his desperate attempts not to perform a complete three-sixty on his projected hover trolley, he managed to knock over Scaremonger's pint, which burnt its way through the counter and the next twelve decks below.

'My...my pint!' declared Scaremonger.

Jimmy did not need to attended a class in "How to Recognise the More Subtle Facial Expressions of Dangerous and Disgusting Alien Life Forms" to realise that Scaremonger was suddenly seething with fury.

'Ooops,' he replied lamely. Scaremonger's hands attempted to thrust themselves through Jimmy's ribcage. Jimmy was helpless to stop himself being hurled backward across the room, kicking numerous Repugnatrons in the head as he went.

It was like someone had stood in the centre of a herd of sleeping bulls and declared, "I'M WEARING RED!" All around, Repugnatrons awoke instantly as the first sounds of a fight breaking out seeped into their heads. Throughout the room, war cries rang out: "Fight!", "Scrap!", "Brawl!", "Half price at Club-U-Need!"

Jimmy made for the door as fists began to fly, the tables would have flown too if the management hadn't got wise to this by now and had welded them to the floor.

'Ali!' he shouted over the noise, 'let's go!'

But Ali was surrounded by angry Repugnatrons and couldn't get past. However, it didn't exactly look like she was trying too hard to escape either. She was swinging the bar's pool cue around her head, screaming like a banshee, sending it cracking off the heads of any Repugnatron who dared get too close. Ali, it seemed, wanted to settle her own score and considered this a down payment.

'Go!' she shouted between attacks. 'Find my brother!'

Jimmy's initial reaction was not to leave Ali in here alone but, if anything, he was actually starting to feel sorry for the Repugnatrons as the disguised GPOL officer was sending many of them slumping back into unconsciousness.

As Jimmy pushed open the door, a beer mug sailed over his head and knocked an oncoming

Repugnatron clean off its trolley with a *thwack!* There were more following up behind, charging down the corridor toward the bar with a look of bloodlust on their faces - it had worked, the word had got out. Jimmy just hoped it was enough to clear the bridge...

> Back on the bridge

Edison held his breath as Fragnut tuned the view screen into the feed coming from the "Slam and Brag". If all was calm he didn't know what he was going to do; only a fight, it seemed, was enough to distract a Repugnatron from its work.

As the screen flickered into life, a benign, smiling Repugnatron face filled the screen.

'That's not the look of a brawling Repugnatron,' said Fragnut, 'everything's fine!'

Edison's heart sank to the bottom deck; Jimmy must have failed to start a fight.

Then the smiling face seemed to wobble slightly, its four eyes tried to cross themselves and it slipped out of sight. In its place hovered a particularly mean looking Repugnatron who was thumping a splintered pool cue into its open palm over and over.

'Pan out, Lieutenant,' cried Gragnash, 'pan out!'

Fragnut yanked a few levers and the entire room came into view – it was...

'PANDEMONIUM!' screamed Gragnash as the view screen writhed with punching, slapping, poking and throttling Repugna-patrons. 'Let's go, Lieutenant!' he shouted as he sped toward the door.

'But almighty overlord sir – the planet mashing!'

'We've still got thirteen minutes until we get there, plenty of time to lobotomise a few petty officers, Lieutenant! Kickhard, you have the bridge!'

Fragnut wavered for a moment before charging after Gragnash and leaving Edison alone.

> C-Wing, penitentiary block

Jimmy didn't have much trouble finding C-wing, he just asked a passing Repugnatron who was far more interested in getting to the bar brawl than it was in interrogating him as to why he didn't instinctively know. He ran down the row of cell doors, poking his head up to the glass window on each. His heart thumped wildly in his chest as he went from one to the other for every one was empty. Then, just as he was approaching the last in the line, a scream rang out. Jimmy froze, not wanting to look through that last pane of glass. As he listened, he heard a familiar voice.

'No! Please! Not again! I can't take any more! It hurts!'

Not knowing what he was going to find, Jimmy burst in through the cell door. As he entered his eyes widened with shock.

> The Bridge

Edison darted across to the console where he'd unscrewed the access panel to the Neutrino Concentrator on his last visit. The panel was still loose,

216

having only been propped back into place. Reaching into the pouch on his hidden GPOL utility belt, he pulled out the portable computer console. However, it only took a few moments to realise that the systems holographic screen and keyboard were reacting badly to his suit's Repugnatron projection. It was no good - he was going to have to drop the disguise. Casting a wary glance toward the closed door, he turned off the suit and became outwardly human again.

'Oh great,' he said to himself. Once he had turned off his disguise, he realised that he still had the BubbleBag slung over his shoulder with the spare Chameleon suit meant for Perry's rescue – Jimmy and Ali were just going to have to use their initiative to get the hostage to safety.

He sat cross-legged on the floor before the access panel and pointed the portable computer at the small round hole in the centre. He typed a series of commands into the virtual keyboard in order to start up a connection with the Neutrino Concentrator. As he hit the Enter key, a thin shaft of blue light shot out of the rear of the computer and made contact with the panel.

'Bingo!' he said as the computer sprang to life, its screen filling with pages of data from the Concentrator. All that was needed now was to upload the password hack and let it go to work.

Edison ran the computer's file transfer program and uploaded the hack code and a program to reset the Concentrator to display in a language that he could actually read. Having taken just a few milliseconds to transfer, the programs began to run. Above his head on the view screen, gBay opened at the Earth's sale page.

217

The hacking code on the concentrator triggered the "ISC: Retract Bid" option and the screen cleared to show a new message in the centre of the screen:

```
"Please re-enter your password in order
            to cancel your bid"
```

Below the message was a box for entering the password and under that were two countdown timers, one on eleven minutes and thirty-two seconds was showing how long was left in which to cancel the sale, the other showed the time until the Disintegrator reached the Earth's atmosphere and was only sixty-three seconds ahead of the first.

As the hacking code entered its second stage – to break the password – the levers on top of the console began to snap forward and backward in a blur of activity as the system went through all password possibilities. There was nothing more that Edison could do to stop the countdown - it was all up to the hacking program, which he'd already estimated could take up to three hours to crack the code...

Trying his best to ignore the constant "beeps" of yet another incorrect password attempt, Edison turned his attention to the next problem: how to stop the escape pods from releasing and acting as a delivery vehicle for the HDF.

> The "Slam and Brag" Repugnatron bar

Gragnash charged through the door to the bar looking like a child on Christmas morning. Bringing up the rear was Fragnut, who was almost as excited but had one of his four eyes on the clock.

'Lieutenant, bludgeon me a swathe through to that vicious one over there,' said Gragnash, pointing to where Ali was cutting down Repugnatrons like a lumberjack on overtime. 'That one needs teaching a lesson!'

Through the corner of her eye, Ali saw Gragnash coming as a systematic felling of Repugnatrons made its way directly toward her. She turned and faced him as he finally burst through into the circle she'd hacked for herself.

'Impressive work, gruntling,' said Gragnash, 'but you've met your match with me. I'm going to knock you clean off that pedestal you've made for yourself!'

'Oh really?' sneered Ali with complete and utter hatred. 'And what exactly are you going to do that with, bad breath?'

'Don't try and flatter your way out of trouble. No, I'm going to crush you with this!' He reached below for his nine-iron and pulled out...

'A heart shaped cushion?' said Ali in astonishment. The rest of the room, who had stopped to watch this confrontation, burst into spontaneous laughter for at least three seconds, which was as long as it took for them to realise that they were giggling themselves into a date with the Grate-O-Matic.

'Erm, no actually...this!' said Gragnash, and casting aside the cushion (much to the distress of Fragnut) he pulled out the gnarly nine-iron.

'Come on then, you putrid pile of fetid filth!' cried Ali.

'You say the nicest things...'

They began to hover around in a circle like wild animals, staring at each other whilst looking for chinks in their opposition's defence. Gragnash made a few lunges but Ali was keeping it tight - nothing was going to get past her. The Repugnatron began to get more and more frustrated as each of his attacks were neatly parried away by Ali's pool cue, his frustration making Ali smile.

'Don't you dare mock the almighty Repugnatron overlord!' blasted Gragnash, and he swung his club at Ali's head with venom. Ali ducked just in time to feel the wind from the club ruffle her unseen hair, the sudden ferocity of the attack throwing her for a moment. Gragnash frowned — his four eyes must've been playing tricks on him because his club seemed to have passed right through the top of his opponent's head.

He attacked again, this time thrusting his club at her like a sabre. The crowd cheered as Ali twisted out of the way but not quick enough to avoid a glancing blow to the ribs. She let out a cry of pain but came back with an attack of her own, flashing the heavy cue just past the nose of the surprised Repugnatron.

'You're never going to win, Gruntling!' said Gragnash, once again narrowly avoiding a jab from the cue.

'But you're forgetting one thing,' said Ali.

'Oh, and what could that possibly be?' mocked Gragnash.

'That the one thing that separates the Repugnatrons from all other life forms in the galaxy-,' and she tossed the cue up in the air and caught it the other way around, '-is utter stupidity!'

With that, she poked the thin end of the cue at the small lever on Gragnash's trolley that controlled the hover. It fell to the ground with a crash, leaving the Repugnatron's lumpy head just at the right height for Ali to thwack it with her pool cue.

'Say goodnight,' said the GPOL officer as she span the cue around in her hand and pulled her arm back for an almighty swipe. But as the cue swung in, another club intercepted her attack, connecting with her wrist with a shuddering crack. In an instant, Ali fell to the floor in blinding pain. Once the initial agony had lessened, it took her a few moments of quick contemplation to work out the answers to two burning questions. One: why was she no longer hovering but lying flat out on the floor and two: why were the Repugnatron faces staring down at her wearing expressions of what looked like deep shock? It took one look at the smashed control panel on her wrist to answer both questions – the blow had caused a power surge through all of her suits systems and she was very much undisguised.

'Lieutenant,' said Gragnash in a voice that sounded like he'd just opened all his Christmas presents and had got exactly what he'd wanted, 'bring the GPOL prisoner to the bridge. Before we kill her, I believe we're due a re-enactment of the last time her race got in our way!'

> C-Wing, penitentiary block

221

As Jimmy entered the prison cell he couldn't believe his own eyes. There was Perry, sitting in an uncomfortable looking seat with a tin opener in his hand. Behind him was the biggest pile of opened tin cans that he'd ever seen whilst before it was an immense vat of lumpy green liquid.

'More!' demanded a Repugnatron guard, who was thrusting yet another tin into Perry's blistered hands. Perry took it with a whimper.

'Erm, excuse me?' said Jimmy. The guard turned and gave him an angry look. 'Ah, may your belly boils be bursting with bile, comrade,' he added, sticking his thumb in his ear and wiggling his fingers. This seemed to relax the guard, who returned the sentiment. 'Listen,' said Jimmy excitedly, 'I've just heard that there's a brawl down at the bar; you wanna' get down there, it's quite a humdinger!'

The guard's eyes lit up at the news.

'Really? A fight?'

'Oh yeh,' said Jimmy. 'Supposed to be the biggest this century!'

The guard didn't hang around for any more information and within seconds had shot passed Jimmy and out of the cell door. Jimmy heaved a sigh of relief and made his way over to where Perry was making heavy going of opening the latest tin.

'I...I'm going as fast as I can,' stammered Perry as Jimmy approached.

'But it's me! Jimmy!' Perry winced at the blast of Repugnatron speech. Jimmy was beginning to think that being held captive by the Repugnatrons had scrambled Perry's mind when he finally realised that he was still in disguise. Disengaging his anti gravity device and the Repugnatron projection, Jimmy became himself again.

'That's better,' he said, 'I was convinced I was even beginning to smell like a Repugnatron.'

Perry's face sped through a wide variety of expressions before coming to rest on "overwhelming relief".

'Jimmy? Jimmy! I can't believe it!'

'Believe it!' said Jimmy, beaming. 'I haven't got time to explain, we've got to get out of here.'

Perry nodded eagerly and tipped the contents of the last tin into the huge vat before him. As the liquid entered the vat, a bell sounded and a whirlpool sprang up in the centre.

'What's going on?'

'I think it's draining,' said Jimmy, staring at the vile looking concoction as it span around and around.

'You'd better help me out of this cha-' began Perry but he didn't get to finish. With a metallic whoosh, the chair tilted forward and pitched Perry right into the centre of the tumultuous liquid. Jimmy cried out in panic and reached in to try and pull the fast departing GPOL officer out but the resistance was too great and with a thundering slurp, Jimmy was pulled in too and vanished along with Perry below the surface.

> The Bridge

As the password hacking program continued to crank the console levers backward and forward at terrific speed Edison sat on the floor, spending what precious

223

little time he had left either hammering at the keyboard in desperate activity or rubbing his temples in mental agony. Try as he might, he just could not find the section of code that dealt with the release of the ship's escape pods. Every time he thought he'd found the right subroutine, following the logic of the code sent him on yet another wild goose chase to other sections of the ship's operating system.

He glanced up at the screen and stared with shock – the countdown timer was reading four and a half minutes until cancellation of the sale was no longer permitted. His head ached with the incomparable stress of watching humanity's life drain away by the second; every beep caused by an incorrect password was like a foghorn of doom in his face.

Come on, he urged himself, *every second counts!*

Turning back to his portable console he stared at the code, searching through line upon line to try and get something to make sense, to try and find the entry point to the escape pod subroutines.

There, was that something? He placed his finger on the virtual screen and followed the flow of a particular line of code – it looked hopeful but what was that noise? A sound was reaching him, the sound of raised voices echoing up the sewer-like corridor toward the bridge. It was too late - Gragnash was back!

'You can't do this, Gragnash,' said Ali. 'You must turn back now!'

Fragnut jabbed her from behind with the nine-iron to make her move faster.

'Can I not? And why would that be?' replied Gragnash, who turned and lanced Ali with one of his most intimidating looks.

'Because they are innocent beings!' she said, almost screaming at him. 'They've done nothing wrong!'

Gragnash bent so fast to within inches of Ali's face that she cried out with the shock of it.

'I,' he said and poked her hard on the shoulder, 'do,' he poked her again, 'not,' poke, 'care!'

Ali wanted to reply but the pain in her shoulder and the putrid smell of Gragnash's breath made the words catch in her throat.

'Why do *you* care anyway,' said Gragnash dismissively, he had straightened back up and was examining the rot in his fingers absently. 'They're not even your people?'

'It's...my job to care,' said Ali in more hushed tones.

'But then,' said Gragnash, showing no signs that he'd heard her reply, 'you haven't got many of your people left, have you?' The Repugnatron's face twisted into a cruel grin. Ali leapt toward Gragnash in fury, the only thing keeping her from smacking all four of his eyes into the back of his head was Fragnut, who walloped her across the shoulders with the club. She fell to the floor with a yelp of pain.

'Nice work, Lieutenant – you've earned yourself an hour off when this is all over.'

'Why, thank you sir!' replied Fragnut, clearly pleased with his reward.

Having hauled the fallen GPOL officer roughly to her feet, the three continued down the corridor toward the bridge. It wasn't long before the door appeared just before them.

'Did you say something, Lieutenant?' asked Gragnash.

'Erm, no almighty overlord sir,' said a puzzled Fragnut.

They came to a stop just outside the door and stared back down the corridor in the direction in which they'd come – there were more voices bouncing up from the blackness beyond.

But not just voices, thought Ali, splashes too, splashes as of someone *walking* through the waterlogged corridor – Repugnatrons do not walk. Her heart seemed to twist around in her chest as she waited for the newcomers to catch up and as soon as they did, her suspicions were confirmed.

'Perry!' she cried, tears welling up in her eyes. 'Are you okay? Are you hurt?'

She made to run to meet him and Jimmy as they were led up the corridor by a Repugnatron wearing what looked like a chef's hat but Fragnut waved the club at her warningly.

'Almighty overlord sir, Lieutenant Fragnut,' said the hat-wearing Repugnatron. 'I found these two swimming around in the tinned soup; dropped out o' the drain pipe – thought you'd want to be a jabbing of them, sirs.'

'You thought right,' said Gragnash, whose smile could get no wider. 'Very good work.'

'You leave them alone!' screamed Ali.

226

'Now you listen to me, you annoying little...*thing*; I am the supreme overlord of all you see, captain of captains, leader of leaders and I *will* destroy Earth,' said Gragnash with a sickeningly triumphant smile, 'and there is absolutely *nothing* that you, GPOL or your little band of space cadets can do about it!'

Gragnash turned toward the door to the bridge. It swung open with a swish and as it did so, a computer-generated voice rang out:

"Repugnatron gBay password hacked! Please push Activation lever to cancel the purchase of planet Earth."

Gragnash's smile vaporised instantly from his face. On the floor, looking across at him with a look of frozen shock, was Edison whilst just above him on the console was the Activation lever, a large red ball on its top was flashing on and off as it waited to be pushed forward.

For a moment no one moved, everyone held their breath but then Gragnash sprang to life first.

'Stop him, Lieutenant!' he shouted, pointing to the still frozen Edison on the floor. Fragnut sprang forward in response but not quick enough to avoid being waylaid by Jimmy and Perry who had simultaneously leapt upon the flailing Lieutenant, trying desperately to hold onto the hover trolley as it collided with the corridor walls.

In the confusion, Gragnash sped forward onto the bridge. Ali jumped up at him, catching his arm but with one flick, she was tossed across the room like a puppet. As she flew toward the wall, she reached out desperately to grab onto something, her hands finding a chain pulley. She hit the wall with thud, sliding to the floor and yanking on the pulley as she went. Above her head, a cupboard opened.

'Push the lever, Edison!' she yelled from the floor but Edison seemed unable to move.

'His pushing days are over!' snarled Gragnash as he pulled his club out from his hover trolley and sped toward Edison.

'No!' shouted Ali, who was helplessly ensnared in the dislodged chain pulley.

At that moment Jimmy and Perry ran in from the corridor; they'd jammed the hover lever on Fragnut's trolley to maximum and it was now pinning the Lieutenant to the corridor ceiling. They entered just in time to see Gragnash's club waiting to crack down on Edison's head.

'Stop!' cried Jimmy but Gragnash was not taking orders.

'There'll be no getting up from this one,' he sneered and Gragnash swung his club at Edison with all his might. The club landed; Edison's body crumpled as it cartwheeled through the air and landed in a heap at Jimmy's feet.

Over by the wall, Ali was overcome with a dizzy mixture of hatred and shock. Disentangling herself from the chain, she jumped to her feet with a war cry but before she could act on this injection of malice-fuelled adrenaline, another announcement from the ship's computer sent a shock through them all.

"Purchase cancellation window closes in ten seconds...nine..."

Standing guard over the console, Gragnash smiled wickedly.

'Oh dear, looks like you've missed your chance!' he said and let out a bark of laughter.

"...eight...seven...six..."

Then something happened that took them all by surprise. Edison's lifeless body made an odd crackling noise and sparks appeared to dance all over him. Suddenly, with a *SNAP!* Edison disappeared altogether and was replaced by the spare Chameleon suit.

Gragnash stared in astonishment.

'Knock knock,' came a voice.

'Eh?' said Gragnash. 'Who's there?'

He turned just in time to see his very own eight-iron club arcing toward his head.

'Blackout!' said Ali and sent the supreme overlord pirouetting into the air before landing in an offensive-looking pile on the floor. However, as Gragnash unexpectedly vacated his hover trolley, it sprang back and knocked Ali off her feet. She landed some distance away from the Activation lever.

"...four...three..."

No one was within three seconds of reaching and activating the lever and they knew it. For Jimmy, time and sound seemed to distort as he watched the last real hope for his planet's survival slip away. Even his eyes seemed to be reporting delirious information to his brain - it must have been because there was no way that the end section of the Repugnatron control console could've suddenly morphed itself into a person. Could it?

"...two..."

'You've lost!' said Gragnash from the floor.

Jimmy blinked. His eyes were telling the truth. In a microsecond, Edison had deactivated his Chameleon suit's projection of a section of Repugnatron spaceship and had risen to his feet. Just before him was Gragnash's hover trolley, sitting motionless at waist height.

'No,' he said as he kicked the trolley toward the Activation lever, 'we've won, actually.' The trolley zoomed through the air at a staggering speed and collided with the flashing lever, thrusting it all the way forward with a *clunk*.

```
"Purchase bid of item GBMW3141592654:
Planet Earth, has been cancelled.  The
item has been withdrawn.  Thank you for
    using gBay and have a nice day!"
```

On the floor Gragnash let out a howl of anger and defeat; a howl that was mimicked from the doorway as Fragnut hovered in, having freed his hover trolley from the ceiling.

Ali ran over to Edison with a look of elation emblazoned across her pretty face.

'Edison! I thought...I thought Gragnash had...'

Edison shrugged nonchalantly, a small smile playing on his lips.

'He might yet,' he said, motioning his head to where Gragnash was trying to right himself on the ground.

'Lieutenant,' screamed Gragnash, 'kill them!'

'That command has been taken down and will be used in evidence against you, Gragnash,' came a voice from above the console. Ali looked up at the view screen to where it had split itself into two sections. On the left side, the cancelled purchase screen remained whilst on the right the Admiral of GPOL Milky Way was glaring down at the fallen Repugnatron.

'Da-', she started. 'I mean, Admiral!'

Titan's face seemed to almost collapse into a state of anxiety before it tightened once again.

'Officers, are you all okay?'

'Yes,' said Ali, 'we're fine. The humans too.'

Titan looked over at Edison and nodded. 'I hear that Gragnash has "changed his mind" over his purchase of your planet, human. That must be a relief.'

Edison raised his eyebrows. He had his arms folded across his chest and was leaning back casually against Gragnash's ornate chair.

'Yeh; I think he'd bitten off more than he could chew...'

At that moment, the ship's computer raised an alarm.

"Warning: Inbound Matter Transportation Beam, destination unknown."

'It's the Technoids,' said Jimmy. 'They've beamed in the HDF!'

Edison almost fell over himself to get to the portable computer terminal, which he'd hidden under Gragnash's chair.

'What's going on?' said Titan as the section of screen next to the Admiral's image began to fill with commands from Edison's computer.

231

'Indeed – what *is* going on?' demanded an even more confused than normal Gragnash. Ali took it upon herself to explain all the panic-inducing details to those that were out of the loop. Gragnash made an odd squealing noise and flapped his arms around.

'Lieutenant, ready my escape pod!' he screamed.

'I wouldn't bother,' said Edison without looking up, 'you could well choose the escape pod filled with enough explosive to destroy an entire planet.'

Gragnash fell silent and slumped against a console, all four eyes were glazed over and his lips were quivering. On the screen, the face of the Admiral seemed to pale more than usual.

'I...I'll send a ship,' he stammered. 'We can be there in five minutes!'

'Don't bother,' said Edison. 'When the escape pod jettisons, it'll take around two minutes to enter Earth's atmosphere. You'd be too late.'

'But can't the Repugnatrons destroy it once it's clear?'

'No,' said Edison, his hands were still flying across the keyboard and his conversation was becoming stilted. 'Repugnatron weapons are offline when Disintegrator is open. Only chance is to stop pods releasing.'

The left section of the view screen cleared suddenly and in place of lines of system code, an outline diagram of the ship and its escape pods appeared. There were only seven pods remaining.

'I think I've found the code,' said Edison, 'but it looks like you have to lock each pod one at a time.'

232

'No offence,' said Ali, 'but shut it and get locking!'

'No offence taken,' mumbled Edison.   He entered a long command and looked up at the view screen – the first of the seven pods flashed red and a message appeared by its side stating "Release System Locked!"

'One down, six to go...' said Perry.

Edison returned to the keyboard and entered another long command. Looking up, he watched as the second pod flashed red.

'Go on Ed, you can do it!' said Jimmy but Edison wasn't so sure; any second now and the HDF pod would release and would propel itself to Earth and the only thing that he could do about it was taking far too long.

One by one he entered the locking command and secured one pod after another, each one making his hands shake with adrenalin as he closed in on the last remaining pods.

'Come on, Edison,' said Ali, 'last one!'

'That's right,' he said, 'increase the pressure why don't you...'

He risked half a second to stretch out his cramped hands; he calculated that the improvement in finger speed would buy him more time back. As he typed in the locking command for the last pod he cursed as he mistyped a line causing him to repeatedly smack his forefinger on the backspace key to remove the incorrect code. He was about to press "Enter" when an alarm sounded and froze his hands where they were poised.

'Oh, no,' said Ali.

Edison hardly dared to look at the view screen. The last pod was flashing green and was shown moving away from the ship, a message stating "Pod Released" flashed beneath it.

Everyone stared blankly at each other – even Gragnash and Fragnut were lost for words. On the right of the view screen, Titan put his head in his hands.

'Is there any chance that the last pod didn't have the HDF in it?' asked Jimmy.

'It's my guess that they put some in each, just in case of a problem,' said Edison.

'You tried your best,' said Ali weakly.

'Yeh, Ed,' said Jimmy quietly. Edison stared at them all; the image of his mother came to him, busying herself around the house with no idea of the terrible fate hanging over her. He took a deep breath.

'I...I'm sorry about having to do this but...I've got to go.'

'What?' said Ali with amazement. 'Go? Go where? Are you saving your own miserable hide?'

'It's been good working with you all,' said Edison, who reached for his left arm and entered a few commands on the Chameleon's wrist computer. A few seconds later and his body separated into a trillion specs of light, which then shot upward in a MatTran beam, right through the ceiling of the bridge.

Out in space, the escape pod filled with canisters of Hydro Desolation Fluid ignited its engines for a three second burst of power, thrusting it toward Earth's upper atmosphere at tremendous speed.

'I don't believe it,' said Ali, aghast. 'He's actually gone and left us!'

Her heart lurched as she suddenly remembered something that Edison had said to her when she had dropped him off on the hillside after the house explosion: "Rescuing is not my thing." Maybe that hadn't been a joke after all.

'Why are you so surprised,' came the Admiral's voice from the view screen. 'That's exactly why we don't deal with humans!'

Jimmy didn't say a word; his face was completely expressionless.

'It's a good job I won't be around to throttle the life out of you, Edison Fox,' bellowed Ali, 'wherever you are!'

'I'm here.'

They all turned and stared at the left side of the view screen, which was now showing what looked like the inside of an escape pod along with Edison's head and shoulders.

'Edison?' said Ali. 'Are...are you onboard the pod?'

'I've told you before, there's one other way to end this,' said Edison, his face serious. 'Only one.'

'But, Edison,' said Ali, 'the only other way is to hold down the self destruct button...'

'Correct.'

'But you can't!'

'You know I have no choice.'

Ali mouthed unheard words but they all knew it was true.

'I know you can see this feed, Admiral Titan,' said Edison, his image scrambling itself in bursts as he approached Earth's atmosphere. The Admiral nodded

235

solemnly. 'I just want to say that I'm sorry that I've put the life of your family in danger and that in future – if there *is* a future – I hope that you can try and see humans in a better light.'

The Admiral made to answer but a burst of static from Edison's camera stopped him. When Edison's grainy image reappeared, they watched as his arm and unseen hand stretched out toward the self-destruct, sliding back the safety cover and pressing down on the recessed red button. A synthetic voice began a countdown.

"Self-destruct initiated, pod vaporization in ten...nine...eight...seven...six..."

Edison turned from the camera and stared out of the window, it was filled with the gradual sunrise of magnificently sculptured brown-green landmass and the glistening blue of oceans.

"...five...four...three..."

'Beautiful,' he said in an awed voice. 'Really worth looking after...'

"...two...one..."

On board the Repugnatron ship the view of the escape pod's cockpit disappeared and was replaced with an external view of planet Earth. They all watched as a glowing red dot exploded into a million fragments, each one leaving a trail of incandescent yellow light as it entered and dispersed itself harmlessly in Earth's atmosphere, giving all those on the surface that happened to be looking up to the heavens an awesome firework display, the significance of which none would ever know.

Epilogue

> Admiral's office, GPOL Headquarters, two days later

Ali sat before the Admiral's desk; her hands were limp at her side and her stare was threatening to burn the titanium covering clean off the desk's surface. Perry was still resting; his stomach seemed to be giving him a huge amount of trouble since his rescue. It was put down to accidental ingestion of the Repugnatron soup and the recommendation that he have a full colonic irrigation, just to be on the safe side, was not making him feel any better about life.

'Are you listening, officer?' said the Admiral.

'Humm? Oh, yes, sir,' replied Ali, although her stare was still aimed somewhere beyond the paperwork littering the desk.

'If it makes you feel any better, it *has* made a difference,' said Titan.

'Really,' said Ali, with more than just a pinch of sarcasm. 'How?'

'Well for a start, he saved the lives of billions of innocent people. That's not something that everyone can claim.' Ali lifted her stare and aimed it at the Admiral. He sighed. 'And besides that, he even made *me* think.'

'How do you mean?'

'He said that he'd hope I'd see his people in a better light and, to be honest, I have.'

Ali sat up. 'Does that mean you're going to recommend an envoy to invite them into the gBay Treaty?'

'No, I'm afraid not. I'm still of the opinion that they're not ready for that.' Ali let out an exasperated noise. 'However, I have agreed to, somewhat unofficially, "keep a protective eye" on them in future. You never know – they may have potential to be great allies.'

Ali smiled weakly – it was her first in days.

'Now, when you get back from your recuperation, I need you to go and see Crackpot; he's making some ridiculous complaint about stolen memories and gruesome trades. He'd be best to stop pointing the finger and just take his rap, that one.'

'Yes, sir,' said Ali. 'Is that all?'

'Yes,' sighed Titan, 'you may leave.' Ali rose to her feet and walked to the door. 'Oh, and offic-.' The Admiral stopped himself and started again. 'And

Alianna, you did a great job out there. Take some credit for those saved lives.'

'Thanks. *Dad*,' said Ali with an emotional smile, and she left the office.

As she wandered the corridors back to her quarters, she rounded a corner and was almost bowled over by an explosion of red hair coming the other way.

'Oh, Torny, it's you,' she said, knowing what was coming.

'Ali! Are you okay? I heard about your heroic mission - go girl!'

'Torny, use that phrase again and I will laser-shear all your hair off.'

'Okay, okay. So, you still set for me to pick you up tonight for our date?'

'Torny, say that again and I will laser-shear your *head* off.'

'Oh,' said Torny, downcast, 'okay.'

'What've you got there, anyway?' she added, pointing at the box under his arm. Torny became a bit shifty.

'Well, I don't think you'd best see-'

'What is it, Torny? Tell me or I'll laser-shear your-'

'Alright already. It's just...well...it's the remains of the escape pod explosion that the recovery team picked up yesterday...'

Ali looked taken aback.

'There...there were remains?'

'Yeh. Not much, of course,' he said, shaking the box. 'Ironic thing is that they found this bit in Roswell,

New Mexico – what're the chances of that! Lucky we got there first this time.'

Ali snatched the box from under Torny's arm.

'Ah, I'd not be looking in there if I were you – I've got to do tests on the remains and I'm told it contains…urm…body parts.'

Ali looked hard at Torny and then turned her eyes back to the box. Steadying her nerves, she flipped off the lid. Inside was what looked like a charred metallic egg-like object with something attached to it. Rubbing the side, she saw lettering beneath the dirt.

'H…O…L…' she said and rubbed some more, 'T…R…A…N,' she spelt out as the rest of the letters presented themselves. As she rubbed more dirt away, additional text could be seen. 'Property…of…UPS.'

She stared at the charred device with wonder before rubbing at its odd attachment – it seemed to have been fixed with some sort of high-temperature resistant duct tape. With startling realisation, she recognised the attachment – it was a finger.

'Ugh!' she exclaimed but then a flash of colour gleamed through the dirt and sparked her curiosity. Rubbing at the end, she uncovered a bright purple fingernail.

'What…No! *No way!*' she said as the realisation of what she was looking at sunk in.

'Hey,' said Torny with interest, 'that's clever – a hologram projector with a finger taped to it. With its inbuilt anti-gravity generators, you could move that finger around remotely, make it look like you were-'

'-In an escape pod, pressing the self destruct button…' finished Ali, almost breathlessly.

Her father's words came back to her: *"...go and see Crackpot; he's making some ridiculous complaint about stolen memories and gruesome trades"*.

'I don't believe it,' she said. 'He didn't *copy* Crackpot's programming skills – he removed them!'

'Eh?' said a bemused Torny.

'He took them. Then he swapped them back for one of his fingers – he knew it'd grow straight back! And this-', she held up the Holtran device, '-belongs to UPS; Flash and Gordon beamed him onto *their* ship, not the escape pod!'

'Does that mean he's still-' began Torny but his sentence was interrupted dramatically. In a moment that he would later secretly copy onto laserdisc via the office's private Memory Cap machine and play back over and over, Ali dropped the box, grabbed his fuzzy head and kissed him smack on the lips.

The End?

"Martians
Mashed
my
Marigolds!"

Turn to page 17...

Eiffel Tower sold!

"It's mine!"
says crazy American

Full story page 4!

The Daily Tribunal

Friday, June 22, 2012

Gone with a Flash!
Could this be a Ming Die-nasty?

Just three weeks after having installed their long awaited "Flash Gordon" waxwork display, Madame Tussauds is holding lengthy enquiries both internally and with the police after their bouffant blond space hero was sensationally snatched away in the middle of the night. Early indications are that the police have absolutely no credible evidence to go on despite the entire event being witnessed by night watchman, Jack Daniels.

"My shift started thirty minutes before closin' that day," mumbled Jack. "I saw nothin' unusual, sept' for this smug lookin' kid with a, quite frankly, disgraceful t-shirt on. He was hangin' around the Flash Gordon display for ages until I decided enough was enough and I put down me copy o' the Beano and went to boot him out. Only, he'd gone and just where he'd been loiterin' was a big blue 'n white vase, which I'd never seen before. It looked kinda' Chinese...

Jack's account then becomes somewhat fanciful. "Next thing I knew, I was woken- urm, roused into a higher state 'o alertness by a noise from above. Lookin' up I sees this curly head stickin' in through the skylight.

244

Bus Drivers Tire Of Tyre Taking Tyrants!	Bad Case of Gas Makes House Hot Property!
Turn to page 12	Full story page 2!

Then I sees a sight that made me copy of the Dandy shake right out 'o me hand: floatin' above the floor toward Flash was his arch enemy - Ming the Merciless!"

But, asks the Daily Tribunal, what deadly device did the evil moustachioed one threaten our hero with - a ray gun? A Doomsday weapon? "A shoulder bag!" declared Jack adamantly. "He drops this bag off his shoulder 'an pops it over Flash's head!" Sounds like a bit of a squeeze, remarked the Daily Tribunal. "You'd think!" replied Jack. "But the more Ming pushed, the more 'o Flash vanished into the bag until all of him were gone! Then, Ming slings the bag over his shoulder again and whoosh! He's only gone and floated up through the bloomin' skylight and away!"

Numerous other rumours, such as Jack's subsequent return to the Whisky Drinkers Over-Appreciation Clinic and Flash's handover to two large men in black, who had landed their badly driven UFO on Madam Tussauds' roof, are unsubstantiated at present.

This heinous crime leaves the Daily Tribunal with a thought-provoking question: with Flash Gordon gone, who now can we look upon to save us from the ever-present threat of alien misbehaviour? It looks like another hero is required, apply planet Earth, Milky Way...

ABOUT THE AUTHOR!

As a terribly famous author (ahem...) I thought it'd be good if you leant all about me by reading a recent interview. Unfortunately my kids were the only ones available to ask the questions. Sorry.

Me: "Go on then, ask me a question!"

Elliot: "Can I go on the PlayStation?"

Me: "No; ask me about how I've been writing stories for around ten years."

Luke: "Daddy, can I dress up as a monkey?"

Me: "No Luke, you can't – how about you ask me how I've worked as a chef, a mechanic and a computer programmer?"

Katie: "I'm a fairy princess!"

Me: "Yes, you are but why don't you ask me about how I like writing funny books as well as exciting action stories and magical fantasy books?"

Elliot: "Well can I play on the Wii then instead?"

Me: "No. You could ask questions about how we live in Staffordshire and love walking in the forest?"

Luke: "I've got a question, daddy!"

Me: "Ooh, great. What is it?"

Luke: "You're not as good as JK Rowling."

Me: "That's not actually a question. Go and dress up as a monkey."

Katie: "Daddy?"

Me: "Yes, Katie?"

Katie: "I'm not Katie, I'm Fairy Princess!!"

Me: "Right. What, Fairy Princess?"

Katie: "I've got chocolate up my nose."

Me: "That's it. I give up..."

Printed in Great Britain
by Amazon

78560203R00149